Published by Ink
www.inkubatorbooks.com

Copyright © 2024 by Jessica Huntley

Jessica Huntley has asserted her right to be identified as the author of this work.

ISBN (eBook): 978-1-83756-425-5
ISBN (Paperback): 978-1-83756-426-2
ISBN (Hardback): 978-1-83756-427-9

PROLOGUE

25th January 2004

Vera's cheeks and forehead were on fire and sweat beaded on her upper lip. Her whole body was damp, the fever raging through her immune system, sending it into overdrive. She licked her cracked lips, summoning some much-needed moisture to her mouth, but it wasn't enough. She picked up a nearby glass of tepid water and took a sip, her throat screaming at the action, but she was grateful for the small amount of relief it brought her mouth.

She hated being ill, even at the best of times, but it always sucked that little bit more when she was sick on her birthday, especially such an important one. Her mother always told her that when she turned sixteen she'd be a woman, no longer a little girl. Today was that day. And, to make her birthday even more special, she got to share it with her twin brother, Kevin, who she adored with all her heart and soul. He was her rock and the only person on earth who she could wholeheartedly say she loved. She wouldn't survive without him. Usually, as twins, they shared most things, including illnesses, but Kevin had somehow managed to avoid catching the flu, the lucky bugger.

Vera had been in bed with the virus for almost two days on the advice of the local doctor, who told her that with rest and fluids she'd improve in no time. She just needed to allow her body to fight on its own, no antibiotics would help. For as long as she could remember, on their birthday every year, she and Kevin would go for a long walk, no matter the weather. Then, they might stop in the village and grab a soft drink from the pub or maybe a bar of chocolate to share from the corner shop. But her illness had cancelled those plans this year, and an aching sense of guilt made her feel even worse. She'd been hoping she would feel better by now so she and Kevin could celebrate together, even if they had to skip the long walk, but she'd been locked in her room the whole day and it was almost midnight now. Spending their birthday together made it a special occasion, because they didn't have any friends around here since their parents had taken them out of school almost a year ago and decided to home-school them – although that implied their parents had an interest in their education. They didn't. Their home-schooling involved cleaning and chores. Their parents' reasoning had been that there wasn't anything they could learn in school that they couldn't teach the kids themselves.

Her temperature was still high, but a steady stream of paracetamol four hours apart ensured it didn't climb any higher. It had gotten bad, though. At least she was no longer hallucinating and seeing swirling patterns on the walls. Last night, she could have sworn a huge demon visited her while she slept. It may have been her father. She wasn't sure.

Despite the frigid January temperatures outside, the window next to her bed was open to allow the air to circulate. Vera's body kept switching from being too hot to too cold. One minute, her teeth were chattering and the next she was pulling off her layers, fearing she'd self-combust.

She laid back against her sweaty pillows and listened to the rain outside. It was getting late, which meant her birthday was almost at an end. She could hear her parents moving around downstairs getting ready for bed. Her father was drunk again, and her mother was shouting at him. Things never changed in this house, even though she prayed every night that they would. Her father continued to drink and take out his frustration on her and Kevin, and her mother continued to ignore what was happening, telling them it was their fault for being such ungrateful children.

They lived in a beautiful house, in a beautiful village, in a beautiful area of the Cotswolds. Her father worked a decent job in Gloucester, earning enough money for them to get by comfortably. But Vera and Kevin often went without food and new clothes because almost every penny earned went into his drinking and the upkeep of this house. They weren't considered a priority in their father's eyes. And in the community, he wasn't a well-liked man, he was often rude to people and always on the verge of being drunk.

A quiet knock at the door made her look up. It was too gentle to be either of her parents, so it could only be one person.

'Come in,' she said with a weak croak and then coughed.

The door opened and Kevin poked his head around the side. 'Dad's on one again. Can I hide out here for a bit?'

'Sure,' said Vera with a smile. She pulled her legs up so he could sit at the end of her bed. Kevin had shaggy hair, something Vera always teased him about, but it suited his face, which was looking more grown up every day. They used to be the same height, but in the past year Kevin had shot up. He hadn't yet filled out, so he was a skinny lad with a deep voice. It freaked her out sometimes.

'It's freezing in here,' he said, rubbing his arms up and down. 'How are you feeling?'

'A bit better, I guess.'

'You hungry?'

'Not really.'

'Good, 'cause there's nothing much for dinner anyway. I uh ... got you something.' Kevin pulled a small bracelet out of his pocket and handed it to Vera. It was silver and had one small charm attached: a key.

'Thank you. It's so lovely. I'm sorry, I didn't get you anything.' They'd never swapped gifts before as they'd both agreed they didn't want or need anything except each other.

'It's okay.'

'Where did you get it?'

'That doesn't matter. Do you like it?'

'I love it. Thank you.' Vera slipped it on her delicate wrist and turned it from left to right, watching as the dim light from above made it sparkle.

'Will you promise me something, Kevin?' asked Vera, keeping her voice low.

'Yes, anything.'

'Promise me that no matter what happens, we'll always have each other. We'll always look out for each other. We'll always protect each other. No matter what.'

Kevin's eyes grew dark and he lowered his gaze to the

bed, studying the design of her bedspread. Had she said something wrong? Granted, she probably loved him more than he loved her, but she always thought he'd have her back.

Eventually, Kevin nodded slowly. 'I promise. You and me forever. Now, hurry up and get better. I'm bored of Mum asking when you'll be well enough to clean again.' Kevin got off the bed and moved towards the door. Vera could tell he wanted to say something more, but he didn't get the chance.

The door swung open and slammed against the wall, only missing Kevin's face by a couple of inches. He jumped back and hid out of sight in the corner behind the door as his father stormed into the room, eyes blazing and fists clenched.

'Where is it?' he demanded.

Vera pulled the sheets further up to her chin. 'What are you talking about?'

'The bracelet I gave your mother is missing. Where is it?'

Vera's mouth turned to dust. She quickly slid her left hand under the sheet. 'I haven't seen it.'

'Don't lie to me,' he said with a hiss. He stomped further into the room. 'It stinks in here, girl. Have you even had a shower since you've been lying in your own filth? And I pay good money to heat this fucking house. The least you could do is keep the windows shut!' He pulled the window closed with such force that the picture hanging on the wall above Vera's head fell.

She shrieked as it hit her, raising both arms above her head in defence. She knew it was the wrong move as her father leapt towards her and grabbed her wrist, squeezing it so tight she thought it might snap in half.

But she didn't make a sound.

'Thief! You stole it!'

'No! I didn't ... I didn't ...'

'Don't lie to me!' With his other hand, he slapped her across the face. The noise his open palm made against her cheek sounded like a gunshot in her head. The room spun as her vision distorted and she fought against the urge to slip into darkness.

Vera opened her eyes and saw Kevin cowering in the corner behind the door, shaking his head. She didn't blame him. If he got involved, then he'd be beaten too. They'd both learned to stay put and not make a sound when the other was beaten. It wasn't worth them both taking their father's brute force.

Her father hit her again. And again.

His fists pummelled into her weak body like he was tenderising a piece of meat. She wasn't sure how much more she could take. She'd been hit before, many times, but this was the worst yet.

She must have blacked out at some point.

Time seemed to skip ahead.

When she next opened her eyes, she was standing in the middle of her room, surrounded by silence and darkness. Her head pounded and her body was drenched in sweat, her nightgown practically soaked. The sweat ran off her forehead and into her eyes. She could barely see.

A light was on in the hall.

'Kevin?' she called out. 'Kevin, what's happened?'

Nothing made sense.

She stepped forward but stopped when her bare toes touched something wet and slippery. Before she could steady herself, her feet slid out from underneath her and she landed with a hard thump on her bottom. Her hands shot out to the sides. When she brought them up in front of her, they were covered in a dark viscous liquid.

'Kevin?'

Her heart rate doubled as she scrambled to her feet, but the pool of what she now knew to be blood on the floor made it difficult to grip. She crawled towards the door, her knees getting tangled up in her nightgown. When she reached the landing, she saw bloody streaks in the carpet, as if someone had dragged something heavy along the floor.

Her vision swam in and out of focus. The house was quiet; all she could hear was her own racing heart, which pounded like a drum in her ears.

'Kevin!' Her throat felt like it was being ripped to shreds by barbed wire.

No one answered.

The house kept its silence.

PART I

1

Elle

24th January 2024

I don't feel safe in my own home. It's always been that way for me, ever since I can remember. The only place in the house where I feel as if I can breathe without suffocating is down in the damp, dark basement, even though it smells musty and has an enormous hairy spider living in the far corner. It's so big, it could easily overpower and kill a mouse if it needed to. I call it Trevor. I'm not sure how he got to be so big.

I've created a safe corner in the basement, behind a moveable shelving unit. I can pull it out from the wall and squeeze myself into the gap. It's where I always hide when my dad threatens to come after me. He doesn't know about my hiding place because he very rarely comes down here.

When I was a child, I could fit behind the shelves easily, but now I'm bigger, a teenager, it's harder to do and there's much less space than there used to be. I've always been slim. No boobs, no hips, just straight up and down like a pole. It's my long legs and arms that have trouble fitting properly. I'm a bit gangling and awkward, almost as if my limbs are too long for my body.

That's where I am now. In my safe space.

My hair falls across my face like black curtains, so I blow it away and it moves like spindly cobwebs and then I twirl it around my fingers over and over. It's a habit I've had for a long time, so I have a lot of short strands of hair and split ends where I keep pulling it out. I'm not sure what it is about the repetitive movement, but it soothes me. Hearing that snap as a strand breaks is addictive and oddly enjoyable. Most of the time I don't even know I'm doing it. Not until my dad shouts at me to stop fiddling with my hair, or my mum moans at me that all my hair will fall out and I'll end up with a bald spot. But, after a few minutes, I go right back to playing with it.

I listen to the faint sounds above me. It's a Saturday and my dad usually works all day, leaving me to have some time to myself. But today he has a day off and is spending it in front of the television watching rugby, but since his team is losing, he's on the rampage and keeps throwing things, so I thought it best I stay out of his way, rather than be swept up in his rage and get hit on the head by a flying beer bottle. I've brought a book down here and I have the light from my phone, but I don't feel like reading now. Sometimes I like to sit in silence and listen to the various sounds around me. It's amazing how loud the house is when I take the time to listen. The basement especially seems to have a life of its own. Creaks and groans echo from all four corners and sometimes, if I listen hard enough, I can hear Trevor scurrying across the floor. It's nice to have his company. I wouldn't say we're friends, but at least I'm not alone down here. Sometimes I hide for hours at a time. Once, I hid in the basement for almost twenty-four hours, only finally coming upstairs when I needed a wee. I'd taken food and water down with me but forgotten about a bucket.

I'm counting the days till my eighteenth birthday. I still have a long way to go – two hundred and sixteen days – but once I'm eighteen, I can legally leave home and never have to see my parents again. I'd miss my mum, I suppose, but it's a small price to pay to be free from my dad.

I was seven the first time he hit me and, for the past decade of my life, I've been living with his abuse. It's not every day. Some days he's even a decent dad and takes me out to places to buy things like make-up and clothes, but then he laughs at me and says that make-up makes me look like a whore and my clothes make me look like a slut. What's wrong with a crop top and leggings? My mum says I look gorgeous, no matter what I wear. She tells me to make the most of my young, blemish-free skin while I can because soon the lines and wrinkles will appear and age will start to creep up behind me, and then I'll be chasing that youthful look for the rest of my life.

I want to be a fashion designer when I grow up, but my dad won't let me go to college or university. He says I need to get a real job instead, but the only job I can get around here is stacking shelves or working behind a bar, which I'm not legally allowed to do yet. I'm fed up with being trapped in this house. My dad controls my whole life. He even monitors my phone, and I don't have access to Wi-Fi unless I ask him, and he can switch it off whenever he wants. I don't use my phone a lot anyway. I don't have any friends, not since Sarah moved away last year. I miss her. We haven't spoken since she left. She promised me we'd speak every day and never lose touch, but she lied. She never messaged me back when I asked her how she was getting on in her new school.

I finished school last year, but I didn't get very good grades. My dad says they weren't good enough for me to be accepted to college or university, so I may as well stay here with him and Mum. But that's not my plan. I plan to leave as soon as I'm legally able to. Mum will be okay without me. She gets hit sometimes too, but if she cooks and cleans for him, he leaves her alone. Whereas I like to argue back. It's my downfall, Mum says. I should just keep quiet and agree with him, but my rebellious teenage side is too strong to ignore.

'Elle!' My dad's voice booms above me, sending small cascades of dust down on my head as he stomps up and down across the floor.

'Stay quiet, Trevor,' I say, pushing my finger against my mouth. 'Shhh!' Trevor doesn't answer. He never does.

'Elle! Where's that fucking girl?'

Every muscle in my body screams at me to stay as still and quiet as possible, but my brain is telling me the longer I hide, the worse the beating will be when he finally finds me. If I come out now, maybe it won't be so bad.

I wait two more minutes before crawling out from behind the shelves and dusting myself down. A few of Trevor's webs tickle my face, so I wipe them away. I wish I could be a spider and live down here in the dark, spinning webs all day, instead of going upstairs and facing the daylight and the mind-numbing dread that something bad will happen.

As soon as my feet touch the top step of the basement, the door is yanked open and my dad glares at me, his eyes wide and his jaw clenched. Not good.

'What were you doing down there?'

'Looking for something.'

My dad narrows his eyes before lunging forwards and grabbing my left arm. He pulls me with so much force that I lose my balance and stumble against his hard chest. He's like a brick wall. He hits like one too.

'Don't lie to me,' he says through gritted teeth.

'I ... I wasn't ...'

Smack!

His open palm slaps across my left cheek. It immediately burns, and tears spring to my eyes. I always try not to react because it only spurs him on, but sometimes it really hurts and tears come whether I want them to or not.

'You make me sick,' he says. He spits at me, and the warm thick mucus hits the side of my face. I wipe it away. 'You should be fucking grateful that you've got a roof over your head, girl. I work hard for this family and you can't even come when I call you. I have to search the whole fucking house for you.'

'I'm sorry, Dad. I didn't hear you down there.' My voice is a low whimper when really all I want to do is scream at him and spit back in return.

'Whatever,' he mutters. 'Where's your mother?'

'At work, I think.'

He snarls in disgust. 'It's mental to think of that woman working. The only thing she's good for is cooking and cleaning, and the same goes for you.'

My dad is the ultimate sexist pig. It's like he's stuck in the 1950s. He thinks all women should stay home and look after their men. This is wrong on so many levels, I don't even know where to begin. The one time I told him this, I was locked in my room for three days, only being given water and bread once a day. I had to use my wastepaper basket as a toilet. It wasn't a pleasant experience, one I never want to repeat, so now I continue to keep my mouth shut.

'Well, since she's not here, you best get lunch started.' He turns and walks back towards the lounge where the television is blaring away. 'Oh, and get me a beer from the fridge.'

I head into the kitchen. It's fairly clean because Mum tidied it before she left for work this morning. I'm envious of her because she gets to escape this house for a few hours at a time and I don't. I miss school. I didn't get good grades, but that's because I purposefully struggled so that I had to stay behind and do extra homework. In hindsight, I should have done better and then maybe I could have secretly applied to colleges and universities, but all I could think about at the time was spending as much time away from this house as possible. I didn't think about what bad grades would do to my future career.

Now, I'm stuck here with no prospects, no way of earning money, and am doomed to become my dad's slave when my mum inevitably leaves him, or he kills her by pushing her down the stairs. That's why I'm counting the days till my eighteenth birthday. I just hope I make it that far.

I open the fridge and grab the last bottle of beer. While walking to the lounge to deliver the bottle, I keep my head down, wishing I was invisible. I hold it out to him, but he just stares at me with a blank stare.

'How am I supposed to drink that?'

I forgot to open it for him.

Without saying a word, I return to the kitchen and search for the bottle opener. It's usually in the drawer beside the fridge, but it's not there. Maybe he has it on the table next to him, but I dare not go back and ask, so I try and open it using the side of the worktop. I use the sharp edge of the cap and wedge it into the wood, then with one sharp tap, I knock my palm against it. I have no idea what I'm doing, but I try again anyway.

The bottle slips from my hand as the cap pops off. I freeze on the spot, knowing that the shit is about to hit the fan. Cold, frothy beer soaks into my socks but I barely feel it. All I feel is the tingling of fear as it creeps up my spine and into my brain. My brain is telling me one thing – to run – but my muscles won't respond.

My dad barrels into the kitchen. He doesn't say anything. He simply lunges at me with his fists clenched.

'Dad, I'm sorry!' But there's no point in even trying to beg for forgiveness. I raise my arms as a shield and take the hit and the next one, and the next, until I collapse into the beer and shattered glass on the floor. I don't even feel the pain, but I do smell the pungent aroma of beer. It's all I can do to not gag. I've always hated the smell.

'Clean this up, then go and get me another six bottles. You have fifteen minutes.'

Tears mix with the beer which splashed against my face when I fell into the puddle. Slivers of glass embed themselves into every available area of my bare skin, my hands and ankles mainly. But the sting of pain is nothing compared to the sheer explosion of hatred and anger coursing through my veins.

It's not directed at my dad. It's directed at me.

Why am I putting up with this abuse day in and day out? I don't deserve it. I'm a good kid. I do as I'm told for the most part. I don't take drugs and I don't drink alcohol. I'm still a virgin. Sort of. I don't deserve to be treated like a slave by my dad, who never deserved to have a daughter in the first place.

Mum told me once that I was an accident. After she spent a few days freaking out, she eventually decided that she wanted to keep me, but my dad wanted her to have an abortion. Figures. People should have to take some sort of test before they're allowed to have and raise children, because my dad definitely would have failed that test. He should never have been a father. I think he is the way he is because of his own dad. He doesn't talk about him much, but the few snippets of information he has let slip tell me that his dad wasn't a nice man. Like father like son, I suppose.

I slowly stand up, avoiding stepping on any more shards and fetch a dustpan and brush from the side cupboard and begin to sweep up the broken glass. Then I mop up the beer using kitchen towels because I can't find the mop and bucket. As I walk over the tiles, my socks cling to the sticky substance that's now drying on the floor.

I leave it and head upstairs, not even bothering with a shower. I've made up my mind. I know where Dad keeps his spare cash. He thinks I don't know that he squirrels cash away from my mum. Between the pair of them, I'm surprised they can even afford food for the table and a roof over our heads with the amount they fritter away on pointless things. I grab the whole wad of cash, not bothering to count it, then head to my room and begin shoving some clothes into my backpack. It was a gift from my mum on my first day of school. Back then, it swamped my small frame, but now it snuggles against my back perfectly. It's a little frayed and damaged in places and there's still a dark red stain from when a pen leaked ink inside it, which makes it look like blood, but it's the one thing I use every single day. I take it everywhere with me, and now it's about to carry everything I have in the world to wherever I'm about to go.

I can't stay in this house another minute. If I don't leave now, I might say or do something I regret and then my dad will take it too far. I've ended up in hospital twice before, lucky to have survived his beatings. Mum told the doctors and nurses that I'd fallen down the stairs and they believed her. No one has ever checked up on me. Not even my teachers when they see me with a black eye.

I'm fed up with being invisible.

My dad is back in his armchair. I don't even stop and look back at the house as I storm down the front path. My feet turn instinctively in the direction of the town centre. There's a bus station there. I have everything I need in my bag, including a fake ID that my friend Sarah got for me a year ago as a leaving gift. Apparently, her brother knew a guy who knew a guy. I didn't ask any questions. I haven't even used it yet. Until now, I've had no use for a fake ID, not being a drinker. The name on the ID is Eleanor Spencer, but my real name is Elle Walter. Elle isn't short for anything. It's just Elle.

I stroll past the shop where Dad buys his beer, and my brain starts doing that annoying thing and imagining how mad he will be when I don't come home. Then I start to laugh, even as the heavens open and the rain soaks into my hair. I pull up the hood of my rain jacket which I'd remembered to grab on the way out and approach the lady at the bus station tills.

'Where to?' she asks me.

I stare up at the departures board, searching for a town I recognise. 'Can I just have a minute?'

'Sure. Can you step to the side please so I can serve the next person?'

I take two steps to the left. This is silly. I can't do this. I can't run away from home. What the hell makes me think I can survive on my own with only a handful of cash, a fake ID and the clothes in my backpack? Then I catch my reflection in the window next to me.

The left side of my pale face is swollen, my hair is still sticky from the beer I rolled about in and there are scratches across my cheeks from glass slivers. All this because my father beat me. All this because I accidentally broke his last beer bottle.

'No more,' I say to the reflection.

I look back to the departures board and see the name Barrow-on-the-Water and a flicker of recognition ignites in my brain. Wasn't that where Sarah moved to?

I'm pretty sure it is. I remember her telling me it was considered the most beautiful village in the Cotswolds. It might be a good place to start. I just need somewhere to lay low for a while, a few weeks or maybe months while I get some more money together. I need a job, a place to stay and maybe someone who won't treat me like something they scraped off the bottom of their shoe.

I need somewhere my dad won't look for me. I've never mentioned the village to him, even when Sarah moved away, so there's no reason he'd look for me there. I know Sarah has never messaged me back, but I'm sure once I get there, I can track her down. It can't be a big village.

It's the only plan I have, and I'm going for it.

I turn to the bus ticketer. 'One ticket to Barrow-on-the-Water, please.'

I'm on my way to freedom and a brand-new life.

2

_____

Vera

Heavy raindrops pelting against the kitchen window create the most soothing of sounds. No matter how tired, overwhelmed or frustrated I am, when the rain comes, it wipes it all away, even if only for a moment. Early morning rain is the best, or during those nights when my overactive brain keeps me awake. Most nights I sleep soundly, like the dead, but recently I've had a lot on my mind. Racing thoughts and anxiety spin around making me dizzy and they're difficult to shut out. Sometimes it feels as if I'm riding a rollercoaster of emotion. The up parts are manageable, but the down parts are when I retreat into the darkness of my mind, and it feels as if I'll never come up to the light again. There are bad things buried in there, so I try not to visit too often. That's why the rain helps. The noise dampens the voice inside.

You're a bad person.

The negative self-talk pipes up, reminding me how truly damaged I am. I've always been damaged, never fully healed from the trauma of my young life. It's not my fault and some-times I must remind myself of that.

I place the mug of coffee on the table and wrap both hands around it, enjoying the warmth against my palms. I don't know why I drink coffee because I don't even like it, but I need the caffeine to get me through the long days as a self-employed cleaner, and my other part-time job of packing boxes and stuffing envelopes.

I service the nearby Airbnbs. There are dozens in the area, all of varying sizes. Tourists flock from all parts of the country to stay in this picturesque location in the Cotswolds because it's considered the most beautiful village in the county. I'm not sure when it was awarded that acclaimed title, or who judges these things, but the village of Barrow-in-the-Water is often in the papers because of its outstanding natural beauty and chocolate-box cottages, complete with huge cascading hanging baskets on every corner of every house along the main high street. Spring and summer are obviously the most spectacular times to visit and that is when the village receives the most tourists.

However, it's almost the end of January now, so the area is quiet, which means not as much cleaning work for me. I struggle to make ends meet as it is, which is why I don't declare all my earnings to HMRC. Once spring makes an appearance then my hours will increase, but that won't happen for several months. Sometimes I am forced to make a choice between eating decent food and paying the bills. If only this house wasn't so big and expensive to run.

Dawn House is enormous. Twenty years ago, it stood

proudly between two large oak trees next to a babbling brook, like something out of a romance novel or a country magazine. But today, it is in ruins and looks more like a haunted house attraction. Over the years, I've had to turn off the heating in a lot of the rooms to reduce the bills, and make judgement calls whether to pay to fix a broken window or seal a room off completely. The once light stone walls are now dark grey, almost black, and crumbling in places. The climbing ivy on the left side has completely taken over, growing in between the cracks, and pushing apart the concrete blocks and creeping up and over the roof tiles.

I was born in this house, and I think it's inevitable that I'll die here too. I can never sell it. Within its walls are the memories and mysteries of my whole life. This house is a part of my soul. Without it, I would lose my purpose in life. Parting with it is not an option. It holds too many secrets.

My eyes flick up to the clock on the wall. I need to leave for work in ten minutes. Only one cleaning job today; two hours' pay. Not enough to cover this week's food bill. But I have to keep going. I can't afford to give up. I'm no quitter.

I stand and pour the dregs of coffee down the sink before turning on the cold tap and rinsing away the dark liquid. The stainless-steel sink has seen better days. Despite having a cleaning job, I struggle to keep on top of cleaning my own house. When I get home from work, the last thing I want to do is clean this place. Also, my Henry hoover broke two months ago, and I don't have the money to replace it, so the carpets are filthy and covered in black cat hair. Luckily, my cat doesn't come inside very often – it could definitely be worse.

Although it's a stretch to call Ollie my cat. He's a stray who adopted me roughly five years ago. He isn't a cuddly cat, nor is he housetrained, so I installed a cat flap which enables him to come and go as he pleases. Sometimes he'll curl up in front of the log burner in the colder months and sometimes I won't see him for weeks at a time. His jet-black fur is surprisingly shiny, but I've noticed he's getting a few tangles around his neck. If I had to guess his age, I'd say he must be ten or so. Ollie is my only friend and, despite him not being particularly friendly, I do look forward to his visits. Even if I could do without the fur embedded in the carpets and the disgusting dead animals he drops on my doorstep from time to time like an offering.

As I shrug into my warm jacket and grab my keys, a low thud echoes through the house. This house seems alive at times. Creaks, groans and thuds sometimes catch me off guard, especially during the night. I often wonder if the house is haunted, but I'm not sure I truly believe in ghosts. Not in the physical sense, but this house certainly has echoes of long-forgotten memories, which are just as frightening as a ghost. If these walls could talk ... Well, luckily, they can't.

Because the secrets inside these walls can never get out. The ghosts within the walls can never be allowed to roam free. They must stay trapped here forever. This means I must stay trapped here too. Forever. Maybe I'm the ghost who haunts Dawn House, doomed to remain alone until I can repent for my sins on my death bed.

But I'm still young. Not even middle-aged yet. My thirty-sixth birthday is tomorrow, although I look fifty-six and feel seventy-six. My body has carried the weight of my choices for twenty years and it's added decades to my demeanour. I've always felt that my name was more suitable for an old lady, and now it feels appropriate. I was named after my grandmother, who I'd never met, but my mother told me she'd been a terrifying woman who enjoyed tormenting her about her weight.

The idea of staying where I am and doing this day in and day out for the next thirty-six years (or for however long my body and mind hold out) is enough to give me heart palpitations. Living like this feels like I'm constantly climbing a mountain, pulling a boulder behind me. I'm not sure how much longer I can keep living this life and keep this house running. But I can't let it go. I can't. It's not only my life that depends on it.

My left hand reaches to the delicate silver bracelet encircling my right wrist. A birthday gift from many years ago, from a time I'd just as soon forget. Tomorrow is the twenty-year anniversary of that fateful night. It's always a difficult day for me. I'm glad I was able to fix the clasp after it broke. The bracelet has barely left my wrist since. I can't even drown my sorrows, having never touched a drop of alcohol. There's always a first time, of course, but alcohol is one of those experiences I've never wanted to take part in. I saw what it did to my dad over the years. It changed him from a bad man into a monster; a monster who destroyed his family one bottle at a time.

Another thud rattles the house around me. Time to leave for work. My eyes flick to the door at the end of the hallway. I bow my head, say goodbye to the ghosts and walk out into the rain towards my car, which is practically on its last wheels. I'm surprised the frame hasn't fallen apart completely. The back left window is stuck in with gaffa tape and the engine refuses to start on cold mornings. It only just scraped through its MOT last year, so this year I'm expecting it to fail. If it does, then I'll sell it for scrap and make do without a car. It's a luxury I can't afford.

The garden path leading from the front door is severely overgrown and uneven. The cobbles have worked their way loose over the years and weeds have grown and spread across the whole area, adding to the look of a long-abandoned building lost in time. Twenty years is a long time to let a garden grow without taking care of it. I don't have the money for a gardener, nor the time or energy to manage it myself. I feel sorry for Dawn House. It was once so grand and beautiful. Now, it's a ruin.

Just like me.

3

Elle

The bus journey from Gloucester town centre to the village of Barrow-on-the-Water takes almost two hours because of all the stopping and starting, but I enjoy the gentle hum of the engine, the chatter of passengers and the vibrations of the vehicle as I stare out the window at the passing countryside. The roads become narrower and windier the further we travel away from the city and my stomach flutters with nausea, but it's also an exciting feeling. I've never been outside of Gloucester before, so my eyes soak up every road sign, building and wide-open field and river I see. I never realised how beautiful this area is before. Years ago, my parents would take me a few miles outside of the city to a nature reserve and we'd have a picnic, but that's as far as I remember venturing. They were never fun trips, always ending up with Dad screaming at me or Mum for something or other.

When my feet finally step down from the bus, I feel a little dizzy. I haven't eaten since breakfast and it's now almost four in the afternoon. I left home at one. Dad must be going crazy by now. Mum won't be home yet unless he's called her and told her that I've disappeared. Maybe he's noticed his cash stash is gone. Then he'll really be mad. While I was on the bus, I counted the notes I'd stolen from him. I have £785 to my name, which sounds like a lot to me. I'm pretty sure it's the most money I've ever held in my hand, but I know from how much my dad complains about the state of the economy and how much food costs, that money doesn't go very far these days, although I can't help but think his money would go further if he actually used it to pay for food and utility bills rather than booze. I try not to dwell on what his reaction will be at finding his money gone as I walk down the high street, attempting to put one foot in front of the other. It feels as if I've walked a thousand miles already.

The darkness of the early evening has swallowed the whole village by now, so I can't make out a lot, apart from the array of boutique shops and cute cafés, most of which are about to close for the day. The drizzle of rain has now turned into a torrential downpour, soaking my leggings and jacket as I walk, searching for shelter. It's cold and uninviting and suddenly a sinking feeling in my gut makes me question whether this was the right decision after all.

Technically, I'm homeless until I find out where Sarah lives. Where do I even start? I call her number again even though I know it won't connect. This is the biggest and most reckless decision I've ever made. I hardly ever do anything on the spur of the moment, unless you count the time I grabbed a chocolate bar from the shop counter and ran out without paying because I was fifty pence short. But even then, I returned the next day, admitted what I'd done and handed over the fifty pence. The shop keeper just looked at me as if I was boring him to death.

I realise that I should have booked myself a hotel room or something on my phone while I was on the bus, just in case I didn't find Sarah straight away.

Right at that moment, the bus drives past me on the way out of the village and sends a torrent of water splashing over me. I shriek and just stand there, staring after it.

Then, silence envelops me.

And that's when I realise the truth: I am totally alone here.

I try and stifle a whimper as I tighten the hood around my face. I look up and down the road, trying to decide which direction is the best option, but neither looks particularly inviting. The village itself is deserted of life.

My stomach grumbles. I need food and water and a place to stay. I can't see me managing to find Sarah tonight, so I turn left and start walking slowly up the road, keeping my head down against the wind and rain. My mind starts shifting through all the silly mistakes I have made as a teenager. Like the time I cut my own bangs, and that time I thought drinking a litre of Coke was a clever idea. But this far outweighs all those mistakes. This is easily the stupidest thing I've ever done, but all I know is I am glad to be away from my house. In a weird way, I feel safer here, alone, than I ever did in my own home.

There's a small shop up ahead, so I shuffle through the door and out of the rain. I pick up a sad-looking sandwich, a bottle of Coke and a bar of chocolate; the dinner of a teenager. As I'm paying, the old man behind the counter gives me the once-over and I feel an anxious knot form in my stomach.

'Um, please can I use your bathroom?' I ask.

The man points behind him. 'Down there. Turn right.'

'Thanks,' I mumble.

After I've done my business and washed my hands, I check out the state of myself in the grimy mirror. My hair is plastered to my face and a dark bruise is beginning to form around my left eye. It's not too swollen at the moment, but it's tender to touch and I wince as I trace its outline.

As I walk down the aisle back towards the door, I feel the old man's eyes on me, almost as if he's judging me. The rain hasn't stopped; in fact, it's increased, and the temperature is dropping by the minute. I check my phone, as if I'm magically expecting Sarah to have called me back, but instead there's a voicemail from my dad. The sight scares me so much that I immediately switch the phone off and stuff it into my pocket. Out of sight, out of mind.

I have no idea where I'm going, but as I shuffle up the pavement, my eyes sting with tears. They mix with the rain, so it's hard to tell how much I'm crying. I stumble across an overhang, perfect for keeping out of the downpour, so I huddle underneath, pressing myself against the door at the back. It doesn't keep out the wind, but at least I'm out of the rain, although it's a bit pointless now, since I'm soaked through anyway.

I remember walking through Gloucester town centre and coming across a homeless person, wondering how they ever let their life get to such a desperate state. Now, I know better. It's because they had nothing left. I think how they must have been forced into that situation because they'd been let down in the worst possible way.

I sniff and wipe my runny nose with the back of my soaked jacket.

'What the hell are you doing squatting outside my door?' A loud female voice makes me shriek and I leap to my feet as a woman carrying a large umbrella appears in front of me. It's hard to make out her features, as the darkness shields her face, but she's dressed in a proper rain jacket and boots.

'I-I'm so sorry,' I stutter. 'I was just ...'

'Look, you can't stay there. What will people think? Who are you, anyway? You don't look familiar.'

'Um, my name's El ... Eleanor.' In the nick of time, I remember my fake ID. I'm no longer Elle Walter. She no longer exists.

The woman lifts her chin up and studies me closely. 'You're not from around here, are you?'

'No,' I say, unsure how much I should tell her. I need to make sure I don't tell her too much that will give me away.

'So, why are you here squatting outside my building?' asks the woman. I notice she hasn't introduced herself yet. This isn't exactly the best place for a conversation either.

'I ... I didn't realise it was a house. I just needed some-where to keep dry.'

'Well, like I said, you can't stay there all night, can you? Where are you from?'

'Um ... Bath,' I say quickly.

'How'd you get here?'

'On the bus. It dropped me off about half an hour ago.'

The woman looks me over again, taking in my soaked clothes, wet hair and pathetic demeanour. I feel about an inch tall. 'What brings you here?' she finally asks.

Why is she so interested in my background? Is this normal stuff for a person to ask a stranger? She seems overly nosy, and it's making my stomach flutter with nervous butterflies. I've never been a big talker. In fact, I've never had a person ask so many questions and be so interested in me before, but I get the feeling she doesn't actually care about my wellbeing. She's just wondering why a pathetic teenager is huddling here.

'I ... um ...' Shit, I can't think of a good enough back story as to why I'm here, so I splutter out the truth before I realise what I'm saying. 'I'm looking for a friend of mine who moved here about a year ago.'

'What's their name?' she immediately retorts back.

'Sarah Lowther.'

The woman shifts the large umbrella to her other hand. 'I don't know anyone by that name.'

I shrug. 'That's okay. Thanks anyway.' I'm not sure why I'm thanking her. She hasn't been helpful to me at all so far and is coming across as rude. I step out into the rain. 'I guess I'll see you around.' I take five steps along the pavement and then she calls out to me.

'Wait.' She almost sounds bored, as if it's an effort to be doing this. I stop and turn around to face her. She walks up to me and stands close, holding the umbrella over both of us. 'As it happens, you're in luck. I have an Airbnb room that's available this week. It was supposed to be rented out, but the bastards cancelled last minute. I didn't give them their money back, of course. It was too late for a refund, but the room's clean and ready to go. How much money do you have on you?'

I gulp at the abruptness of her question, but the thought of a dry place to stay the night is enough of an incentive to see how this plays out. 'I have some money,' I mutter.

'How's fifty quid a night sound?'

'Um ...'

'Just until you find your friend. I need the room back at the end of the week. I have more people staying, so you'll need to get out by then.'

I look around at the heavy rain and darkness just as a gust of wind catches the umbrella and almost rips it from her hands. I don't have any other choice. Despite her prickly tone, she is offering me a roof over my head and protection from these ferocious elements. She could have told me to bugger off somewhere else, but she hasn't. Maybe it is my lucky day, although it doesn't really feel like it right now.

'Yeah, thank you. That sounds good.' Good, but fifty quid a night sounds like a lot of money. It won't take long to burn through the cash I have. But is that the going rate? I have no idea how much a room costs to stay in overnight. It's the first time I've stayed away from home on my own.

'Well, come on then. Let's get you out of this weather. What's your name again?'

'Eleanor.'

'I'm Laura.'

I nod in response. She turns and starts striding up the pavement, leaving me standing in the downpour. I'd assumed we'd be going inside this building, but apparently not, so I half jog to keep up with her. She doesn't offer to share her umbrella and she doesn't slow down to allow me to catch up either.

After about ten minutes of this, she stops outside a small semi-detached house. I watch her wordlessly as she fumbles with her keys and kicks open the door, muttering something about how it always sticks when the weather's bad. A ratty little dog rushes towards me as I step over the threshold, and it stands there yapping in a high-pitched tone.

'Don't mind Hamilton. He doesn't like anyone,' says Laura as she takes the umbrella down, shakes it and stands it upright in the corner.

I close the door behind me, shooting Hamilton a quick look. It's not that I don't like dogs, but when one clearly doesn't like me, it's hard to feel any sort of positive emotion towards it.

Laura takes off her jacket and ignores me completely. I feel like a fish out of water. Maybe spending the night out in the cold rain would be better after all. Then again, the warmth in this house is already heating up my insides. I need to get these wet clothes off and dry them somehow.

Laura eventually turns and looks at me once she's put her boots away. Now she has her hood down and her jacket off, I can see that she's quite pretty and young. Maybe mid-thirties, but she has a lot of hard lines around her eyes, like she's worked a lot of late nights.

She shakes her head, like she can't believe she's let a homeless girl into her house. 'Fifty quid for the night,' she says, holding her hand out.

'Um ... okay.' My hands tremble as I reach into my pocket and pull out some of the notes, which are a bit soggy. I hand her fifty pounds, which she counts, as if I'm going to short-change her. Then she nods up the stairs in front of me.

'Room on the left at the top. Bathroom's opposite. Use the dark blue towels, not the white. If you want a proper breakfast, then it's at eight, but it'll cost you a fiver extra.'

'Breakfast sounds good,' I say because the idea of a

proper breakfast makes my mouth instantly fill with saliva. 'I'll see you in the morning then.'

'Sure,' she says. 'If you want a shower, then turn the knob all the way to the left, otherwise the water will be too cold. Oh, and if you hear strange noises in the night, it's probably just the dog. And there's no lock on the bedroom door, so you might want to put a chair under the door handle.' Then she simply walks out of the room without bidding me goodnight. I stand awkwardly in the hallway, wondering how the hell I've wound up here.

Hamilton growls at me as I take a step towards the stairs.

'Down boy,' I say.

The wooden stairs creak as I walk up them, dripping water as I go. As I push open the door, I hold my breath, wondering what I'm about to walk into, but to my relief, the room is clean and tidy. I look out the small window onto the street below, which is lit up by a few sporadic streetlights. There are small rivers running down the sides of the road, flooding sections where the drains are blocked. It's quiet too. Not many cars or people milling about.

Despite being out of the rain, I still don't feel comfortable or safe, but it's better than wandering around in the dark for the whole, long night. At least now I'll be able to get some sleep and start afresh with my search for Sarah in the morning after a decent breakfast.

I peel my soaking clothes off in the bathroom and step under the running water, letting out a satisfied sigh as the heat warms my internal body temperature. Once washed, I wrap a dark blue towel around my chest, pick up my clothes from the floor and step into the hallway, ready to sprint across the landing to my bedroom.

Hamilton is blocking my path. He's sitting right outside my bedroom door, staring at me.

'Um ... can you move?'

A low growl emanates from his throat.

'Look, can you move so I can get to my room?' I take one step at a time, my eyes locked on the dog who's ready to pounce at any moment. His little yellow eyes watch me as I slip inside and slam the door in his face.

Ha!

Elle, one. Hamilton, zero.

I do as Laura suggested and shove the wooden chair in the corner underneath the door handle, although the idea of Hamilton reaching up a paw to open the door sends a smile to my lips; the first one I've had since arriving here.

The radiator is on, so I whack it up as high as it will go and drape my wet clothes over it, hoping they'll dry out enough to put back on tomorrow morning, then I crawl under the sheets.

I thought I'd fall asleep straight away, considering how tired I am, but deep sleep eludes me. The small bedroom Laura has put me in is comfortable and warm, but the weird noises outside the door make it feel like I'm trapped in some sort of underground bunker. Is that really Hamilton pacing up and down or something else? Despite my makeshift lock, it's not enough to make me feel safe from whatever is lurking in the corridor. Instead, I teeter on the edge of slumber, have a few vivid dreams where I'm being chased by an invisible monster, then jolt awake as I fall off the edge of a steep cliff into the choppy waves below, breaking every bone in my body.

Eventually, I succumb to sleep and the next morning I wake to the smell of bacon, something I've never experienced before. Usually, I make my own breakfast and I often choose cereal or peanut butter on toast because it's quick and easy and involves little to no mess or washing up.

A small clock on the opposite wall tells me it's almost eight. I don't want to miss breakfast, so I force myself to get out of bed and check the clothes I left drying on the radiator. They are dry, warm and welcoming.

I get dressed and take down my chair lock, then quietly open the door a crack and peer out.

Hamilton is sitting in the exact same place as when I left him last night.

It's both oddly comforting that I had a tiny guard dog outside my room all night, and mildly terrifying that he seems to be obsessed with me.

'Are you going to let me get past?' I ask him.

Hamilton blinks up at me, but at least he's not growling. Maybe we're turning a corner in our relationship.

I traipse downstairs, following my nose until I reach the dining area. The space looks like it's from the 1850s, not that I know what decor of that era looks like, but trinkets adorn the shelves of the impressive Welsh dresser on one side of the room, and the furniture looks handmade, built with love and attention. I run my hand across the back of one of the wooden chairs, admiring the carvings.

'My husband is a carpenter. He has his own business in the village and sells hand-turned wooden items at the village market.'

I turn towards Laura, who is leaning against the doorway. 'It's nice,' I say, not really sure if it's the right thing to say or not.

'You want breakfast then?' she says, her tone changing abruptly.

'Um ...'

'Bacon and eggs okay?' she asks.

'Sure. Um ... is anyone else staying here?'

'Why?'

'I thought I heard someone walking up and down the hallway last night.'

'I told you. It was probably the dog.'

'I think he slept outside my room all night.'

Laura frowns. 'He must like you. Think yourself lucky. By the way, if anyone in town knows where your friend lives, it will be William Graft. He's lived here all his life and knows everyone in the village. He's a proper nosy bloke, but not always welcoming to strangers. Tell him I sent you. He works at the little shop down the road. It opens at nine.'

'I think I met him yesterday.'

Laura nods once more and leaves the room. I take a seat by the window and look out onto the street. The rain's stopped, but the ground is still soaked. In the light of day, more of the village is visible. A few early risers are walking about, including a young man who opens the butcher's shop just across the road. I study him, immediately drawn to his dark hair and broad shoulders. He looks like he's only a year or two older than me. The butcher's shop is called Porter & Son. Maybe he's the son. It seems like a simpler life here. Family-run businesses and no one running about, stressed about their lives, or shouting at each other. My mind drifts to an image of the butcher boy and me being more than friends and walking down the street holding hands, which immediately makes me feel silly because I don't intend to get close to anyone around here. I can't afford to let my guard down.

After the most delicious breakfast during which I eat until I can't take another bite, I head back up to my room.

Hamilton is nowhere to be seen, and I find myself disappointed that I don't get to say goodbye. I'm not sure if I'll be back here tonight yet. It depends on how today goes. I've got my fake ID on me, the money and my backpack.

I pop my head around the kitchen door, looking for Laura. She's standing at the sink, washing up. 'Um, I'm off now.'

'You staying another night?' she asks without turning to look at me.

'I'm not sure yet. If I find my friend, then no, but if I don't, then yes.'

'Okay.' And that's the end of that conversation.

As I enter the corner shop, the one I came to last night, the bell rings above the door. The aisles are narrow, the shelves stocked full of so many products. There're no other customers that I can see as I make my way towards the counter at the back. An old man stands behind it, his white hair combed back, and thick-rimmed glasses perched on the edge of his nose. He peers over them at me.

'You were here last night.' His tone isn't friendly.

'Um ... Hi, Mr Graft. Laura said you might be able to help me find out where my friend lives.'

'What's the name?'

'Sarah Lowther.'

Mr Graft nods and I feel a rush of relief. 'Yeah, I've heard of her. She moved here with her family a little over a year ago, but they don't live here anymore. They moved again about six months later.'

My heart sinks like a stone and my shoulders slump forwards. 'Oh ... Do you know where the family moved to?'

'No.'

I lower my eyes to the floor as he continues to glare at me over his glasses. Why is everyone around here so unfriendly?

I give him a small nervous smile, which he doesn't return, and then I turn and head outside. As I turn left, I bump straight into another person who's about to enter the shop. I'd been so distracted by the bad news, I didn't even notice him.

'I'm so sorry,' he says.

'No, I'm sorry. It was my fault. I wasn't concentrating on where I was going.' As I straighten up, I realise the person I've walked into is the young man who I saw opening the butcher's shop earlier. My cheeks burn and my heart leaps as he looks at me with his twinkling blue eyes and smiles. It's almost as if he can see into my soul and read my mind. I hope he can't because the image of us holding hands and kissing pops into my head again.

'No harm done,' he says.

Heat flushes my chest as I return his smile. 'Have a nice day,' I say, dipping my eyes and scurrying up the road. After a minute or so, I slow to a stop to catch my breath. I've run off without any sort of plan of where I'm going, so I look around, searching for something to catch my eye and offer me some guidance.

What now?

Sarah doesn't live here anymore, so my whole plan of staying with her is no longer an option. What do I do? Head home with my tail between my legs and accept whatever punishment my dad feels is necessary? Travel to another village or town and try again?

'Hey, wait up. Are you on holiday or have you just moved here?'

My head snaps up at the sound of his voice. The butcher boy has caught up with me – or, I think, was he following me?

'Um ... neither, really. I was looking for a friend of mine, but she doesn't live here anymore, and now I'm not sure what to do. I've recently left home so ...' Shit, why am I telling this guy my life story? He doesn't need to know all that. 'Sorry,' I say, shaking my head.

'No need to apologise. Well, hey, if you want to stick around, there's a job going in the café up the road, and Laura owns an Airbnb you might be able to stay in for a while.'

'Actually, that's where I stayed last night, but she's only got a room available for the next week.' I manage to look at him properly and smile. 'And thanks for the heads-up about the job.'

He smiles at me again. 'I'm Eric Porter.'

'Eleanor Spencer.' The lie slips off my tongue easily this time, almost as if I've finally relinquished my true identity and accepted my new one.

'I hope I see you around, Eleanor.'

My heart jolts as he says my name, even if it is my fake one. 'You too.'

'Welcome to Barrow-on-the-Water,' he adds with a wink.

I watch as he walks back down the road and slowly release the breath I've been holding for the past thirty seconds. He's the first person who has been friendly towards me and his manner calms my shattered nerves. Can I really try and stay here for a while? I could get a job, then I could earn money for rent. I just need to find somewhere else to stay, which I'm sure won't be too hard to do.

For the first time in a long time, hope and happiness bloom inside of me. No more hiding in a dark basement. No more watching what I say in case it's the wrong thing. I can have a life here, be part of the community. It might take some time to get settled, but I truly believe that being here is the right decision. It's a shame Sarah has gone, but now I can make new friends. Like Eric. And maybe Laura. Okay, maybe not Laura.

Goodbye, Elle Walter.

Hello, Eleanor Spencer; a girl who can be happy here.

4

Vera

Since the weather is still bad, not raining, but not warm or pleasant either, I drive into the village. Dawn House is located approximately two miles by road from the centre of Barrow-on-the-Water, or just over one mile by foot. I usually prefer to walk, since it saves on petrol, but sometimes using the car is unavoidable and makes more sense. The only way to reach the village is by either driving down multiple roads with grass growing in the middle of them that are only wide enough for one car or by foot down a tranquil lane which, at this time of year, is ankle-deep in mud. There isn't a lot of petrol left in my old car, but it's better than carrying all my cleaning products through mud. Often, I use the products at the Airbnbs or I'm able to leave my own there, locked in a cupboard, but I have a few bottles of replacement bleach I need to take with me today, and that's why the car is a better option. I'm strong, but carrying bags of numerous heavy bottles through thick mud is not a challenge I fancy.

As I manoeuvre the car down the narrow lanes, being careful of the deep potholes that have gotten progressively worse this winter, I catch a glimpse of myself in the rearview mirror. When did the lines around my eyes get so deep?

Happy birthday to me.

I haven't dwelled too much on the fact that it's my birthday, but I'm determined to do something later after work.

I park in my usual spot around the back of the first Airbnb and begin to unload the bottles of bleach from the boot. I shove an old jacket further into a corner. I found it the other day while I was searching my parents' old bedroom for something warmer to wear, and I thought it might come in useful when I'm out and about, although the idea of slipping my arms into my father's old jacket sends a shiver down my spine. It still smells of him, and it's a smell that turns my stomach. I very rarely go into the extra bedrooms in the house, mainly because there's no reason to. There are six in total. My mother always said she wanted to open a bed and breakfast, but that idea was quickly cut short by my father, who said he didn't want random strangers in his house while he was trying to have a shit. Such a delightful man.

'Good morning, Vera,' says a familiar voice.

I turn around and see Laura, the owner of the Airbnb, staring at me from a nearby doorway. I've cleaned her building ever since she first opened. She keeps me afloat, but sometimes she can be a little bit nosy, so I make sure to keep my distance and my answers to her questions short. Unfortunately, she seems to think it's acceptable to stick her nose into my business every chance she gets. Also, she always has some sort of complaint. Maybe I didn't scrub the toilets well enough, or there was a dust bunny under the bed. Surely, if she was that unhappy with my work, she would have fired me years ago, but I'm still here cleaning the room she lets out. I have no idea why she rents one of her rooms out. Maybe she simply likes the extra income.

She watches me as I get out of my car.

'Morning,' she says. 'A lot of rain last night,' she adds. Is she trying to engage me in conversation? I wish she wouldn't bother.

'Mm-hmm.'

'Did you get any flooding around your place?'

'No.'

'We had rivers of rainwater gushing down the streets here.'

I carry the bottles of bleach in their bags towards her. 'Same service as normal?'

'Actually, no. I know you usually do a deep clean of the bathroom today, but there's a new girl staying for the next few days. Her name's Eleanor. I found her squatting outside another of my places last night. Soaked to the skin she was. Looked like a drowned rat.'

I nod, even though I stopped properly listening after the first few words. My mind often drifts when people are talking. 'Fine. I best get on,' I say.

'Don't know if she's coming back, mind. She needs to find somewhere else to stay by the end of the week. I'm not sure why I decided to offer her the room. I don't often take in strays.'

She's making it sound like this girl is some sort of lost and abandoned dog, not a human being.

I grunt in reply and shuffle past her into the building,

donning my apron and yellow cleaning gloves. I've already tied my hair back in a messy ponytail, so I begin by gathering my supplies together and then replacing the bottles of bleach in the cupboard.

I start cleaning the bathroom first. There's a bed and breakfast cottage down the road that I'm due to clean in an hour, so I can't take too long here. It's almost half past nine now, so by the time I arrive at the cottage, the tourists staying there will have had breakfast and left for the day on their travels around the area. There are some lovely places to visit, so I'm told, but I've never actually been to any of the historical landmarks or nature parks or walked up the nearby hills to look at the views. I can't spend too much time away from Dawn House, which is why I only clean for roughly four hours at a time before returning and checking on the place. The longer I'm away, the more my anxiety grows, like a tumour in my stomach, twisting and causing me painful discomfort.

The main thing I like about this job, though, is that no one talks to me. People see a cleaner and the most they'll say is 'Hello' or maybe 'Have a nice day'. No one cares about cleaners. They're like invisible fairies to most people; they come and clean and leave nothing but a minty-fresh smell and a clean towel perfectly folded. That's exactly how I like it.

I enter the room that the girl stayed in last night. It barely looks as if it's been used. The bed has been made, albeit not up to my standards, and there's only a single tissue in the bin by the door. I cleaned this room thoroughly only two days ago when the last person who'd used it checked out.

A low growl makes me jump. I turn and see Hamilton

standing in the doorway. I ignore him. Hamilton and I have never got on well.

'Oh! Hello,' says a voice I don't recognise. 'Sorry, I just came back to grab my phone. I left it charging last night.'

I almost drop the bottle of disinfectant spray I'm holding. I spin around and see a young girl standing behind the dog in the hallway, peering in at me. She's the most delicate, prettiest thing I've ever seen. Black hair that hangs in curtains past her freckled face, pale skin, oversized hoodie and ... As soon as I see the dark bruising around her eye, I avert my gaze, pretending I don't notice, but my body must give me away. That bruise practically leaps off her face and shouts at me.

I watch as the girl comes in and unplugs the phone from the charger by the bed. She must notice me staring because she says, 'Just a misunderstanding with a door.'

I nod, keeping my eyes down. I wish she'd go away. My anxiety is rising by the second, after seeing that bruise. I know why it's there. Because she's me. She can't be much older than I was when ...

I shudder and turn my back to her.

'Have a nice day,' she mutters. She moves past me and I watch her walk away, wishing I could rescue her and stop her from suffering the way I did. I don't even know the poor girl, but suddenly she fascinates me. The dog follows her down the stairs.

THE NEXT THREE hours pass by uneventfully, yet slowly. I head to the bed and breakfast up the road after I've finished at Laura's. There's a strange stain on the carpet in room six, which I think is red wine. Luckily, using my magic mix of baking soda and cold water, I'm able to remove it from the pale carpet. And someone in room two has clearly shaved their legs in the bath and forgotten to rinse afterwards, so I do the honours. Plus, there's a towel that's covered in ... Well, it's not chocolate, let's put it that way. I sometimes question whether there are human beings or animals staying in these rooms. How people can come and stay in someone else's place, and treat it like a stable is beyond me. I guess they're just counting on leaving it for the cleaner to sort out.

On several occasions, I've had to get Laura, or the owner of another Airbnb involved. Last year, not in this building, but one further out of the village, the people staying there trashed the place; they broke windows, the television, the toilet. Once, I even found a man passed out naked in the bathtub. I managed to wake him up, but then he shouted abuse at me. The life of a cleaner is not a glamorous one, but I do take pride in my work and most of the time there isn't a problem and people are grateful.

I finish all the cleaning by lunchtime, so after picking up bread, eggs, milk and pasta from the corner shop, I drive home on autopilot. My mind is still on the girl I saw earlier. Laura said her name is Eleanor. I remember that much about the conversation. What else had Laura said? Something about her needing to find another place to stay?

As I pull up into the driveway, I take a few moments to stare at the house; my home sweet home and prison sweet prison for the whole of my life. Sometimes I think about taking a match and setting the whole place alight while I stand back and watch the damn house burn to the ground. Then I would laugh and dance in the ashes and say goodbye to the ghosts of my past.

But that's impossible. I can't do it. The house and its

contents mean too much to me. I'm not a bad person. But I've made some bad choices over the years, and they have led me to being imprisoned in my own home.

I park the car and give the door a good shove as I enter my house. I flick the kettle on and open the fridge, scanning the near-empty shelves for something I can make for lunch.

A sound I haven't heard in a very long time chimes through the empty rooms of my home.

My body freezes and the egg I picked from the fridge slips out of my hand, exploding on the floor, covering my shoes in sticky yolk. My heart rate doubles and all the air rushes from my lungs.

The doorbell!

No, no, no, no, no!

Who is that? What are they doing here? Did someone follow me or were they waiting for me to arrive? I didn't see a car anywhere at the locked gate. They must have walked from the village or …

The chime rings again.

And then a muffled thud starts vibrating through the house. Over and over and over.

I spring into action, slam the fridge door closed, ignoring the egg on the floor, and shout, 'Just a minute!' at whoever is at the door. I double-check the door to the basement is shut and locked, straighten my flyaway hairs using the hallway mirror and then peer through the peephole.

Damn it.

I open the door a crack.

'Miss Marks? I'm here to read your electric meter.'

What? Why? I sent the company the readings last month. Granted, I falsified them to save myself some money. Maybe that's what this is about. They think I'm trying to swindle them ... which I am.

'How did you get past the gate?' I demand.

'I walked from the village. Someone told me I'd be better off walking than driving due to the state of the road.'

'Now isn't a good time,' I say.

'Miss Marks, we've sent countless letters and tried calling, but your phone appears to be switched off or you've changed your number.'

I've done both, but better to play dumb.

I open the door a little wider. 'I'm so sorry, but I'm just about to do the laundry.'

'This won't take long. I simply need to do an accurate reading of your electric meter and then we need to sort out a payment plan. Where is it? I can be out of your hair in less than half an hour.'

My mouth opens, but nothing comes out. There's another few thuds, but only I can hear them. Or maybe they exist only in my imagination.

The young man in front of me gives me a frown as he says, 'Our records show that, unusually, in this old house, the electric meter is in the basement. Can I come in and check?'

My left hand is clutching the door so tight that my whole body is rigid. 'I ... I'm not sure that's a good idea,' I manage to say.

'Miss Marks, I really just need to take some accurate meter readings. Due to your late payments, we need to ensure they are correct. If you do not let me in, then I will be forced to get the bailiffs involved, which may even mean it becomes a police matter.' Can he do that? Is that legal? My mind races as I imagine more people turning up on my doorstep. The police are the last people I want here. I don't have any other option. I have to let him in and hope he does his job and leaves without any issue.

I'm blocking the doorway with my body. 'Um ... okay. But I don't have time to talk about a payment plan. I have to leave for work soon.'

The man goes to say something but then thinks better of it. He nods. 'Very well. I'll just read the meter, but I will need you to call up as soon as possible to pay your latest overdue bill, and also to set up a payment plan, otherwise your electricity will be cut off.'

'Fine,' I say.

I allow the man into the house, watching his every move. It's been twenty years since another human being has set foot inside and I don't like it, especially when they're unwanted and uninvited.

I show the electrician into the basement, switching on the light as he slowly descends the steep stairs.

'Be careful of the dodgy step,' I say as I follow him down. The last thing I need is him tripping and tumbling down the stairs, breaking his neck. Although, if he did break his neck, it would postpone the overdue payments some more, but not forever. Eventually, someone from the electric company would come looking for him, and I assume there'd be a record of the last place he had visited. It would be like having a huge sign outside saying, 'He's here!'

I follow him down, my eyes flicking around. He makes a beeline for the left corner where the water tank and meter are, but I stay by the bottom of the wooden stairs, gripping the handrail tight.

I've done a lot of work to this basement over the years, but it still looks shabby and old, and it smells damp. The lights flicker and no matter how many times I've changed the bulbs, they continue to do so, but I dare not call out an electrician to fix them. The floor is concrete and there are numerous shelving units, boxes and pipes littering the corners and walls. The beams above are exposed and there's one small window in the left wall which leads out into the yard. It's not big enough for a grown person to crawl out of ... I've checked.

Less than two minutes later, the man turns around and smiles. 'All done. Thanks so much. Remember, make sure you call up today. If you don't pay by the end of the week then your electricity will be shut off.'

'Okay, will do,' I say with a quick nod.

'Have a good day. I can see myself out.'

I watch him walk up the steps as I remain at the bottom. Once I hear the front door close, my legs give out and I sink to the floor, trembling. I stay there, and I cry my eyes out.

When I finally peel myself off the floor and walk back upstairs, my mind drifts to Eleanor and then, like a lightbulb moment, I have an idea. What if I invited her to stay with me? Not for free, but she could be my unofficial tenant and pay some rent. It's not a sensible idea by any means, and I'd have to ensure I take precautions, but it might help alleviate some of the financial pressure on me. It wouldn't have to be for long. Just until my work picked up again in the spring and the tourists returned to the area. A few months, tops. Laura does it, so why can't I?

It's all I have. I can't afford to have bailiffs knocking on my door, or people from the gas and electric companies rocking up and demanding payment. It's too risky. I just need a bit of extra money coming in for a while. That's all.

I flick the kettle back on, clean up the egg on the floor and then fetch two mugs from the draining board and use one teabag to make two brews. Then I make two ham sandwiches, since I've just broken the last egg, and I make sure to use the butter sparingly as there's only a little bit left. I wipe the metal tray free from crumbs and set one of the teas and one of the sandwiches on it.

I eat my sandwich in silence as I think about my plan and how I'm going to approach the girl staying with Laura.

5

Elle

After realising I stupidly left my phone on charge at Laura's place, I head back and pick it up. While there, I run into a woman who I assume is the cleaner. Seems an excessive expense for Laura to hire a cleaner for one room. Maybe she's just lazy. The cleaning lady barely said anything to me. I guess no one really talks to them a lot. On the way out, I tell Laura that I'll be staying another night or so and she responds by holding out her hand for money. She tells me again that I have to be out by Friday morning.

Since I've now given up on finding Sarah, I decide my next course of action is to find a job and another place to stay. Maybe there's a room for rent somewhere in town. I know I can't stay at Laura's, not that I'd want to, considering her unfriendliness towards me, although I admit she was nice enough to pull me in off the street.

I visit the café Eric spoke about first, but the owner wasn't in, so I'm heading back there now because the waitress I spoke to said he'd be back in two hours, which was almost three hours ago. My stomach is rumbling even though I had a decent breakfast, but I can't afford to blow too much of the money I have on food until I can bag myself a regular wage. Plus, I need to use some of my cash towards Laura's Airbnb room for the next few days and as a possible deposit for wherever I end up staying next.

The café is called Willow's Café, which is a bit odd considering the owner is a man, but I think it might be impolite to ask why. It's a cute place, but I'd call it more of a restaurant than a café. They are basically open all day and serve breakfast, lunch and dinner plus tea, coffee and cake at all hours. There are various paintings on the walls, all of which are for sale, and are by local artists. Some of them are huge and cost hundreds of pounds. I've never been into art. I can admire a beautiful painting of the surrounding countryside, but some of the more abstract paintings go straight over my head. My favourite of the ones I see is of a black Labrador splashing through a muddy puddle, tongue lolling and ears flapping.

My shoulders ache from carrying my backpack all day. I should have just left it in the room when I went back to get my phone, but running into the cleaning lady distracted me. Plus, I prefer the idea of having everything I own on my back. Not that I've got anything worth stealing, but it's the first time I've been on my own and to be honest I don't know who to trust. I've not had any luck with finding a job yet, so all my hopes are pinned on this café/restaurant, especially since Eric suggested it, because that means I know there's a job going here unless it's been filled already. I have at least found out where all the shops are in the village, including the dentist, the bank, and the market square where the local small businesspeople bring in their handmade items and free-range produce every Saturday to sell. There's also a stall for the butcher, the veg man (who's called Josh), and even a stall that sells gin.

The waitress I spoke to earlier spots me and gives me a friendly wave. Her name's Stacey. I raise my hand and approach the counter.

'I told Carl that you came in earlier looking for a job. He's pretty desperate to hire someone so unless you have a criminal record or something, I think you've got a good chance,' she tells me.

'I don't have a criminal record,' I say with a half laugh. Although I do have a fake ID.

'I'll go and get him for you.'

'Thanks.'

A few minutes later, a middle-aged man with a bad dye job and a big smile appears. He immediately shakes my hand and asks me to take a seat in one of the booths. The place is filling up with hungry diners already, and the waitress (who's the only one I've seen) is running about like a headless chicken, doing about five different jobs at once.

'You must be Eleanor. I only have two questions for you. Are you over eighteen and when can you start?'

His abruptness makes me gulp and my mouth turns dry. 'Um ... yes, I'm eighteen and as soon as possible.'

He claps his large hands together. 'Perfect! You're hired. How about you start right now?'

Again, my heart leaps in terror, but I eagerly nod, not

wanting to lose this opportunity. 'T-Thank you so much. Yes, that's great. I ... I don't have any waitressing experience so –'

He waves his hand. 'I don't care about that. As long as you can carry trays, write down orders and aren't rude to the customers then I'm happy for you to learn on the job. It's ten quid an hour and forty hours a week, including three weekends a month. How does that sound? I'll add you to the rota and let you know your shifts by the end of the day.'

I nod. 'Yes. Fine, thanks.' My heart is practically leaping out of my chest at the thought of earning so much money even if it means being on my feet for so long every day. I'm giddy with excitement at the fact I've just got my very first real job.

'Stacey says you've just moved to the village,' continues Carl.

'Yes, um ... yesterday, but I'm in the process of finding somewhere more permanent to live. At the moment, I'm staying at Laura's.'

'Ah, Laura. She's a live wire, huh? Although she always had a soft spot for my daughter, Willow.' A shadow passes over his face. Something tells me his daughter isn't around anymore.

'Anyway, let me give you a quick tour of the place and then I'll let Stacey show you the ropes.'

I follow Carl into the back where there's a kitchen and a service area. Two cooks nod hello at me before hurrying on with their work. The smells are enough to make me salivate and my stomach gurgles. Carl chucks an apron at me; it is pale yellow and has Willow's Café embroidered on the front in blue letters.

'We close at nine. Good luck, kid. Oh, and when you get a chance, can I get a copy of your ID?'

'No problem.' I swallow back the lump in my throat then turn to Stacey.

'Thank goodness I have some help.' She beams at me. 'Can you start by clearing tables two, six and seven?' At this point, I look around at the tables, but none of them have numbers on them. Stacey must sense my confusion. 'Ah, the numbers are seared into the tabletops so you can't see them unless you're standing right over them.' I nod my understanding and she continues. 'All the dirty plates and stuff just go on the side by the sink in the kitchen. Don't be surprised if you get roped into doing some washing up. The dishwasher keeps breaking.'

I smile. 'No problem.'

My heart swells with pride at the fact I'm here, standing on my own two feet, earning my own money, living free from my parents. Now all I need to do is find somewhere more permanent to live and I'll be set. It feels as if the past twenty-four hours I've been caught up in a whirlwind, but I've never been happier to be swirling around out of control.

My home and my parents feel like a distant memory as I get to work clearing the tables and smiling at the customers, who return my smile and some even give me tips, which I'm allowed to keep.

I NEVER KNEW my feet could hurt this much. At least the throbbing ache in my soles overrides my exhaustion. When Willow's Café finally closes its doors at nine that night, I'm so tired and hungry I can barely think straight, but I can honestly say I've had the absolute best first day in my new job despite my feet having their own pounding pulse.

Most of the customers who came in smiled at me and

were polite, but there were some who got impatient when I got a couple of orders mixed up. A local group of older ladies came in and rattled off their orders so fast that I couldn't keep up and I had to keep asking them to repeat them. They complained to Carl, who explained it was my first day and gave me a wink, saying not to worry. Apparently, they're notorious for complaining.

When I handed my ID over to Carl during one of my breaks, my heart was beating so loud and fast I was afraid he'd notice and wonder why I was so nervous, but he didn't ask me any questions and handed it back to me with another wink. It was weird to be called Eleanor all day too. At one point, Stacey kept calling my name and I didn't respond until she came and nudged my shoulder.

I'm due at work again at ten o'clock tomorrow morning, so at least I get a lie-in. I pop into the corner shop on the way back to my room and grab a sandwich. I inhale it before I reach my door. Carl did say I can sometimes grab leftover food at the end of a shift, but I'd have felt a bit weird doing that on my first day. Maybe I will eventually as I get to know him better.

As I trundle up the stairs towards my room, Laura appears at the top and stares down at me. 'I heard you got a job at Willow's.'

'Um ... Yeah.' Word sure travels fast in this village.

'I used to know Willow quite well. She used to help me out around here sometimes,' she adds, as a slight frown appears on her face.

'Oh, that's nice,' I say because I'm still super curious about what happened to Willow.

'She disappeared five years ago,' says Laura, as if reading my mind.

I raise my eyebrows. 'Disappeared?' I walk the rest of the way up the stairs and stand next to Laura. That's when I notice Hamilton sleeping outside my bedroom door. Has he been there, waiting for me, all day?

'Well ...' Laura leans in closer like she's about to tell me a secret. Her eyes are alight, as if she's excited about spreading some gossip. 'You want to know what I think happened?'

'Um ...'

'I reckon she ran away,' she says and then, after a pause, 'or killed herself.'

The abrupt tone of her voice makes me gasp. 'W-Why would you think that?'

Laura shrugs. 'Or maybe her boyfriend offed her.'

I chew on my bottom lip, wishing the floor would swallow me. 'Okay, well ... I'm going to get some sleep. It's been a long day.' I keep my voice steady even though panic is beginning to form in the pit of my stomach. The sandwich I've just eaten isn't sitting right. Laura makes me nervous.

Laura nods down at Hamilton. 'Least you have the dog guarding your room at night.'

'Yeah ... I guess.'

I watch Laura walk down the stairs, then I bend and stroke Hamilton's head. He looks at me and blinks his eyes, then settles back down to sleep.

That night, before my body finally gives in to sleep, I spend two hours tossing and turning.

THERE'S a gentle knock on my door that wakes me. I open one eye and see that it's still fairly dark outside. What time is it? I reach for my phone. It's just gone eight in the morning.

The knock comes again.

I wonder what Laura wants ...

Peeling back the covers, I adjust my pyjamas, which have twisted in my sleep as I hurry across the floor to the door. I move the chair and open it, expecting to see Laura, but it's not Laura. It's the cleaner from yesterday morning. She's wearing the same clothes, and her hair is pulled back in a messy ponytail.

'Um ... Hi,' I say. 'Sorry, I'll be out of the room in about an hour. Can you come back and clean then?'

The cleaner nods. 'Yes, my apologies. But I'd like to ask if you've found a place to live yet?'

Her words don't register straight away. My brain is still drowsy from just waking up. How does she know I need a place to stay?

'I'm ... I'm sorry?'

The cleaner smiles at me, but I notice she doesn't look me in the eye. 'I heard you need a more permanent place to live. I have a large house about a mile from the village, so it's within walking distance. There's a room in the attic that's liveable. I'd like to offer you the room. Is a hundred pounds a week, okay? Also, if you'd like to earn a little extra cash, I have a box packing and envelope stuffing job that I do from home in my spare time that you can help with. It's not exciting but pays good money.'

My shock and confusion must be evident on my face because the cleaner adds, 'Sorry, I know you don't know me. I'm Vera. I live alone in the house, but you're more than welcome to stay. Something tells me you could use a break.'

I notice that her eyes keep flicking up to my bruise. Eventually, I find my words. 'I ... I don't know what to say.' I don't have time to think about it. This woman is offering me a lifeline and I don't have any other choice. I don't know the woman, but already she seems nicer and friendlier than Laura. 'Um ... yes, okay. Thanks, I guess. My name's Eleanor Spencer.'

Vera gives me a crooked smile. 'Great. When can you move in?'

'Is Friday morning okay? I don't start work till midday then.'

'Yes, that would be fine. I'll come and collect you on Friday morning in my car and drive you up there. I don't want you to get lost trying to find the house on your own.'

'Okay.'

Vera nods and then turns and walks away.

I close the door, still too stunned to really form any words or coherent thoughts. Did that really happen? A small jolt of joy flutters in my chest, knowing all my problems are now solved. I have a job. I have a place to live. And I'm beginning to make new friends like Stacey and maybe Eric. Life is going my way for once.

AFTER A HOT SHOWER, I head downstairs for breakfast. Laura is setting a table. She's wearing a blue cashmere jumper with tight jeans and her hair is freshly washed. I'm glad to see the dank and dismal weather has improved and faint rays of sunlight are brightening up the small breakfast room.

'Morning,' I say.

Laura doesn't look up.

'I wanted to let you know that I've found a new place to stay. I'll be leaving Friday morning.'

Laura places two glasses upside down on the table. 'You have? Where?'

'Vera, your cleaner, offered me her attic room.'

Laura doesn't respond straight away and when I look over at her I notice she's stopped setting the table and is frowning. Then she asks, 'Vera offered you a place to stay?'

'Um, yeah. This morning. She knocked on my door.'

'That's odd.'

'Why's it odd?'

Laura shrugs. 'Well, it's just … I've known Vera a few years now and I don't think she's ever spoken more than a few words to me at a time. She keeps herself to herself. Very quiet. I'm not sure if she's shy or if she doesn't like people, but … I don't mean to scare you, but … I'm sure it's nothing. She lives alone in that huge house and has done for over twenty years. Her parents and brother left her all alone many years ago. That's what I've been told. Loneliness and isolation do things to people over time. It eats away at their souls.'

I'm not sure why, but I feel the urge to defend Vera. I don't know the woman, not at all, but her kindness towards me must mean something. I've always believed there's good in everyone. The only exception to my belief is my dad. Even my mum has goodness in her somewhere, underneath the terror my dad has instilled in her over the years. Vera may be an odd woman, quiet and isolated, but she's reached out to me for a reason. So, to hear Laura saying she's weird is enough to set my teeth on edge when Laura herself hasn't exactly been warm and welcoming.

'I'll be careful,' I say. 'She seems nice.'

Laura finishes setting the table and straightens up. 'Nice people aren't always who they appear to be on the outside.'

Her words make my blood run cold. I can't help but wonder what she means by that and whether she's been misled or hurt by someone in the past. Is that why she's so guarded and blunt herself? Because she doesn't want to get hurt by someone who might use her if she softens a little?

'All I'm saying is ... keep your wits about you in that house.'

'Is it haunted?'

'What? No,' says Laura with a laugh. 'In fact, you should consider yourself very fortunate. As far as I know, no one's been inside Dawn House, not in over twenty years.'

6

Vera

The weight on my chest feels momentarily lighter. It's not completely gone but it's light enough not to be truly suffocating. However, the idea of calling up and making a payment today is not an option right now. I'll have to blag it for a little while longer. Just a few more days. I'm sure when another overdue bill arrives in the post, that weight will come crashing back down on me, heavier than ever, but for now I enjoy the temporary relief. Eleanor moving in will give me the extra cash I need to pay off some of my debts. Not all of them, and it certainly won't happen fast, but her being here will mean I can get them under control. I can pay a few missed payments off and keep the hungry wolves – and bailiffs – from my door.

My birthday was yesterday, but thanks to the arrival of that man from the electric company, I forgot all about it. So, after my cleaning jobs are finished, like I have done for the past twenty years, I go to the shop, buy everything I need to make a chocolate cake, and then head home. The ingredients cost more than I can safely afford, but it's a tradition I refuse to give up. Everyone deserves a cake on their birthday. Everyone. Even if I have to make my own and it's a day late.

Once I get home, I start making the cake straight away. I don't have long before I need to leave again for another cleaning job. Then, over the next few days, I'll need to clear the attic room and make it nice for Eleanor. I haven't been up there in years, but I can't risk putting her in one of the lower rooms of the house. The further she is away from any potential noise, the better. Plus, I'll need to install a security camera so I can keep an eye on her movements when she's in the house. I can't have her wandering the halls and going into any room she fancies. I'll need to buy extra deadbolts too or maybe I can find some old bolts in the garage to save a little money.

As the sweet, warm aroma of chocolate sponge fills the house, I sit in my armchair in the living room with a cup of coffee and enjoy the silence. I fiddle with my silver bracelet, turning it round and round my wrist, a soothing habit I've formed to help battle the rising anxiety.

Once the cake is out and cooled, I cut two slices and put them on two plates, add a fork to each and smile at a job well done. The cake is as delightfully rich and moist as always.

THE NEXT DAY, I wake up early, do my usual morning chores and take a bucket full of cleaning products upstairs to the attic room. I've forgotten just how many stairs there are to reach the top. I take a glance at the door of my old bedroom, pushing the memories of that night down into the dark. I haven't been in there since ...

I shudder as the vivid memory floods my mind.

So ... Much ... Blood.

When I reach the attic room, I'm out of breath. Mum and Dad had the space converted into one large room when I was a child, boarded it out and decorated it tastefully. It was used as a playroom, but has since been left alone to gather dust, mould and goodness knows what else.

I switch on the heating, hoping the single radiator still works, which it does even though it makes some strange gurgling noises to begin with. It may need bleeding. There's a little bit of dampness in the far corner, but nothing I can't get rid of with some elbow grease and the right products. I'll need to bring a bed up here, and that means somehow getting it up the narrow stairs by myself from one of the lower rooms. But I'll worry about that later. I'll use the bed in my old room, although that will mean actually entering the room ... something I'll have to work my way up to.

I make a start picking up all the toys from the floor. It feels as if I've travelled back in time. I haven't set eyes on these objects in so many years, but the memory of playing with them as a child comes rushing back. I see some toys that once belonged to my brother and before I can stop it, a sob erupts from my mouth and tears stream down my cheeks.

Kevin.

My twin.

We used to play up here for hours, hiding ourselves away from our parents. It was our safe space then, but as we grew into our teenage years, we stopped playing together and this attic became a graveyard of childhood memories.

Bending over, I pick up a toy tractor. The green paint is dull now; it's covered in dust, the same as everything else up here. I've brought a few black bin bags with me. I should have done this years ago. One by one, the toys go inside the bag, sinking into it like a deep, dark pit.

It takes me several hours to clean the room and at one point I have a severe sneezing fit prompted by the amount of dust that explodes into the air when I disturb some furniture, but, eventually, the space is clear, ready for me to bring up a bed, a side table and maybe a dressing table. There's already a wardrobe in the corner, which I've emptied. It was full of Dad's old clothes, all of which will come in handy.

As I'm carrying the bin bags down the stairs towards the front door, I notice a pile of envelopes on the doormat. I don't know how many times I've asked the postman to put the mail in the small mailbox at the end of the driveway by the locked wooden gate. I'll have to tape a note on the gate again. He must have parked his van there and walked up to deliver the mail. I really don't want anyone coming too close to the house. When I need things delivered, I always leave a note on my order form instructing to please leave the package in the metal box next to the gate. Luckily, most delivery companies abide by this, but my postman is ignoring my wishes and must have climbed over the gate for some unknown reason. Clearly, the chain and padlock and the 'Private Property: Keep Out' sign isn't enough to deter some people.

I mutter a few indecent words as I bend down and scoop up the envelopes. They can only be one thing: overdue bills. Water, electricity, gas, and one from a repair service I had to have done on the roof a few years ago because it was at risk of collapsing if I didn't do something. I receive at least two or

three warnings a month from these companies, but lately
I've been receiving them daily, and they are piling up
because I keep forgetting to take out the recycling.

Every time I see those red words on the envelopes, my
insides clench and a dull ache settles in my stomach. I'm not
sure how much longer I can avoid them. They keep popping
up. There is a particularly nasty-looking one, which says
'Final Warning!' so I open it and scan the page.

It's the electricity company. Since I didn't call yesterday
and pay, they are threatening to switch off my supply
tomorrow.

I sigh. I do have some money that I was saving, but that's
for my car tax, which is due in a week. It looks like I'm going
to have to make a choice between having a car and having
electricity. It's not a hard choice. I can live without a car. I
can't live without power.

Luckily, there's never been a mortgage on this house
because my mum inherited it from her father. I'm not sure
where he got it from, but in any case, I don't have to worry
about mortgage payments – and being evicted for non-
payment – but to run this house is expensive enough.

After I deal with the rubbish in the black bags, I head
inside and call the bloody electric company and give them
what they want. They take my money, but still give me an
earful about keeping up with my payments in the future.

It will be okay, I tell them. I have more money coming in
soon.

7

25th January 2004

Her body was numb. Completely, truly numb. There was so much blood everywhere. In the bright lights of the landing, it almost sparkled and glowed against the cream carpet. Her bare feet were soaked in it and as she took a few tentative steps forward, the blood squelched between her toes.

'Kevin?' she called out. 'Mum ... Dad?'

But she knew they wouldn't answer. This blood didn't belong to her. She felt no pain other than her throbbing headache. Looking around the hallway and landing, she saw blood smears across the walls and banisters, all the way down the stairs. She peered over the banister at the floor below, moving to stand at the top of the stairs.

'Kevin?'

As she took the first step down, her feet slipped out from

underneath her. The blood acted like a slip-and-slide as she slid and tumbled down the steep stairs. As she landed at the bottom with a heavy thud, the wind was knocked from her lungs. She didn't think any bones were broken, but she now had a nasty bump to the head.

She began to cry.

No one was coming.

But someone had dragged something heavy across the landing, down the stairs and out the front door, which was wide open, letting in the freezing January air. Vera's body shivered against the elements, but she couldn't bring herself to move. She knew she needed to, but her muscles refused to respond to the signals in her brain, which were fuzzy around the edges, as if she were looking at the world through rain-spattered glass.

'Vera!'

Her head snapped up at the sound of her name. 'Kevin!'

There he was, standing in the doorway, very much alive, his thick hair plastered against his face, his clothes saturated with water and covered in blood, which looked diluted thanks to the rivers of rain running off him. Her eyes shifted to what he was clutching in his right hand.

'Kevin ... Why are you holding Dad's cricket bat?'

She'd recognise it anywhere. It was a limited-edition bat signed by the entire England cricket team who'd played in the Ashes in 1958, the year her father was born. He'd inherited it from his father and Kevin was due to inherit it eventually too. She and Kevin were never allowed to touch it or remove it from its plinth in the hallway by the front door. It was his holy grail.

But Kevin was holding it, and it was covered in blood and

something else that Vera didn't want to think about. The mere thought of it made nausea swill in her stomach.

Kevin dropped the bat to the floor and rushed towards her. 'Are you hurt?' He began grabbing her arms, her legs, checking for broken bones or wounds.

Vera yanked her arm out of his grasp. 'Kevin, what the hell is going on?'

'You don't remember?'

'No, I ... a little, but ... my fever is so bad, I can't work out what's a dream and what isn't.'

'You're shivering ...' He placed the back of his hand against her forehead. 'And you're burning up. I need to get you cleaned up and back to bed.'

'Where's Mum and Dad?'

'Vera ...'

'Where's Mum and Dad!'

Kevin lowered his eyes to the floor. 'Dead. They're dead, Vera.'

She heard the words, but they didn't make any sense. How could they be dead? They were alive only a few minutes ago. Weren't they?

Vera glanced at the grandfather clock by the front door. It was gone one o'clock in the morning. How had she suddenly lost almost two hours? When Kevin had entered her bedroom and given her the silver bracelet it had been around eleven. She automatically reached for her wrist, but the bracelet was gone. She remembered her father grabbing it and ... nothing else.

'H-How?' she stuttered.

'Vera ...'

Vera looked at the blood-covered bat on the floor. He

didn't need to say anything else. He had killed them to protect her.

Vera closed her eyes, her fever at boiling point. Nothing made sense. She needed to help her brother. They needed a plan.

'Don't worry, Vera. It'll be okay. I'll keep you safe, I promise.'

Vera nodded. She believed him, but she needed to keep him safe too. He'd murdered their parents in cold blood. What if he killed someone else?

8

Elle

The next few days pass by in a blur of dirty plates, sore feet – and tips. I can't say the work is exhilarating or life-changing, but it's hard, honest work, and I'm feeling more and more relaxed as the days wear on. It's Thursday afternoon, which means tomorrow morning I move into my new accommodation, Dawn House. Laura's warning hasn't put me off and Vera and I have shared a few pleasantries in the corridors as we've passed each other; both of us on our way to do our jobs.

Laura's right in one way, though. Vera is a bit of a loner. She's hard to engage in conversation. I'm not the most talkative of people, mainly because I haven't had the opportunity to talk to people outside of my own family for so long. I find it difficult to keep the conversation flowing with her. She seems distracted somehow, like she has other things on her mind or always has a place she needs to be. Her eyes constantly shift sideways, like she's searching for an escape route.

The ding of the bell above the café door alerts me to the arrival of another customer. My heart leaps as I set eyes on Eric. He's wearing a checked shirt with the sleeves rolled up and a padded gilet. His attire throws me slightly because I assumed people stopped wearing gilets, like, twenty years ago. His work boots have seen better days and his jeans fit him so snuggly that it's difficult to look away. Now that I look at him properly, he looks much older than me, possibly in his early-to-mid-twenties.

I'm halfway through clearing a table and setting it up. He catches my eye and I offer him a quick wave, feeling my face burn, before turning my back to him.

'Hey,' he says.

I spin around to face him again. 'Oh ... Hi!'

'You got the job then?'

'Oh, yes ... Thank you. I've been meaning to pop by and say thanks for the heads-up, but I literally started the minute I got the job, so ...'

'Don't worry about it. I'm glad I could help. Did you manage to find a place to live?'

'Yes, I did, thanks.'

He raises his eyebrows. 'Ah, that's great. So, I guess that means you'll be hanging around here for a bit longer.'

'I guess so.'

'I'm glad.'

'Me too.' My heart is racing so fast I can barely breathe.

'When do you move in?'

'Tomorrow morning.'

'Ah cool.' He smiles. 'You should pop by the butcher's

shop today after your shift, or maybe I can pick you up later and show you around the village. What time do you finish?'

Holy crap, is he seriously asking me out on a date?

'Um ... at five.'

'I'll see you then, Eleanor.' I smile and nod. He flashes me another of his megawatt smiles. 'Is Carl out the back?'

I can only nod.

I stare open-mouthed at him as he walks through the door into the kitchen area. I'm assuming he does it a lot. Maybe Carl buys meat from the butcher's for the café.

'O.M.G., girl! Did Eric Porter just ask you out?'

I snap out of my daze and turn to Stacey. 'I don't think it's like a proper date.' My face heats up at the thought of spending time properly alone with him.

Stacey winks. 'He likes you; I can tell.'

'How old is he?' I need to ask.

'Twenty-three.'

My heart sinks slightly. An age gap of five or six years wouldn't be so bad, but technically I'm still seventeen, not eighteen and a half like my fake ID says, and right now it feels particularly large.

Stacey is looking at me more thoughtfully now. 'Just, um ... be careful, okay?'

'Huh?' I reply stupidly.

'Eric can be a bit of a lad. You know what I mean? Also ... ah, never mind.'

My heart sinks even further. 'Yeah, thanks. Don't worry, I can handle him.' And it's true – I've had run-ins with boys like him before. Although, I guess he's not considered a boy anymore. He's a man. And that's a thought enough to make my mouth dry for the rest of the day.

During a slow moment, Stacey and I are washing

dishes in the kitchen, and I take the opportunity to ask her a question that's been nagging me since I started working here.

'What happened to Carl's daughter, Willow?'

Stacey pauses for a second and then lets out a sad sigh. 'Ah, Willow. I miss her. She was a good friend of mine, you know. We're the same age, went to the same school. One day she just disappeared.'

'Did she run away?'

'Yeah, that's what the police think.'

'What does Carl think?'

'He's convinced something bad happened to her, but there's no proof of anything like that. However, when it first happened there was talk in the village that she may have had an argument with her boyfriend ... with Eric.'

My eyebrows shoot up. 'Eric was Willow's boyfriend?'

'Yeah, but there was no suspicion that he was involved in any wrongdoing. Look, you saw – him and Carl are still good mates.'

I don't get a chance to ask anything else because the chef comes over and tells us it's ten minutes till the afternoon rush starts. I put Willow to the back of my mind and focus on the more important issue: my date with Eric ... or my not-date with Eric. There's a slight uneasy feeling in my belly about the fact Eric was Willow's boyfriend, but if her dad is friends with him, then surely he can't hold any hard feelings towards him. I decide to give Eric the benefit of the doubt. How could I not with those eyes?

FIVE O'CLOCK ARRIVES and Eric walks through the door barely five seconds late.

'Have fun,' says Stacey. 'Tell me everything tomorrow, won't you?'

'I will,' I reply with a nervous laugh. I grab my jacket and attempt to smooth out my hair as I approach him. He's wearing different clothes than this morning. Maybe, as a butcher, he needs to change and shower a lot, otherwise he smells like raw meat. But, as I get closer to him, I smell the sweet tang of aftershave. He's made an effort. And I've just walked off an eight-hour waitressing shift. I probably stink and I'll definitely look a complete mess.

'Ready to go?' he asks.

'You bet.'

He holds the door open for me and then we walk side by side along the pavement. I have no idea where he's taking me, but I feel safe in his company and enjoy listening as he tells me about his job working for his dad and how he's going to take over the family business one day.

I don't say a lot, other than asking him a few questions here and there. It's dark outside and I feel a bit disorientated as he leads me through some gates and along some narrow, overgrown paths.

'Where are we going?' I finally ask.

'Oh, sorry, I should have said,' he replies with a laugh. 'I thought I'd show you the secret garden.'

'The secret garden?'

'Yeah, it's a place where the local kids hang out mainly. We won't be able to see much in the dark, but now you know where it is, you can visit any time you like. I used to come here a lot with ... Ah, never mind. Anyway, here we are.' Eric pushes at a rickety wooden gate and holds it open for me.

He's right. We can't see much in the dark, but from what I can see in the moonlight and the ambient light from the village nearby, it's a wildflower garden with multiple benches and paths.

'So ... Eleanor, what made you come to Barrow-on-the-Water? You said you were looking for your friend.'

'Yeah, but she's moved away now. It's no big deal. I hadn't seen her for a long time anyway.'

'Where are you from then? You know, where'd you grow up?'

My heart rate creeps up as I realise I'm going to have to start spinning my web of lies. 'In Bath. My parents wanted me to go to university, but I wanted to take a gap year instead.'

'Most people go travelling abroad during their gap years.'

'I need money first. My parents can't afford it.'

Eric nods. 'I admire that, you know. You're working to save money all by yourself in a strange place. That takes guts.'

I'm glad he can't see my face heat up and turn red in the dark. 'Thanks.'

A few seconds of silence pass.

'Where did you say you're staying after Laura's?'

'Um ... I didn't, but I'm staying with Vera. She says she has a room in the attic I can use. Do you know Vera?'

Eric and I reach a bench and take a seat side by side. 'Yeah, I know Vera. She always buys the cheapest cuts of meat. Doesn't say a lot, does she?'

'No, I guess not, but she seems friendly enough.'

Eric stares ahead into the darkness in silence. I wish I could read his thoughts. Does he think he's made a mistake in asking me out? Am I too immature for him?

'She lives alone in that big house, you know.'

I guess he's not thinking about me after all.

'Yeah, I know. Do you know much about her?'

'Not really. Just what my dad's told me. She's lived in that house all her life. Her parents and brother used to live with her, but then they moved to Australia, I think.'

'Australia? Wow, that's a bit of a move. Why'd they go there?'

'No idea,' he says with a shrug.

I bite my lip. I can't keep asking him questions about Vera. It seems wrong, like I'm snooping on her or something. I'm sure she and I will learn more about each other soon.

Eric and I spend the next hour talking about this and that and he tells me about the time he almost cut his finger off using the meat saw in the butcher's shop. We share some laughs and, by the time he drops me at Laura's, my mind is so giddy that I don't even have a chance to get nervous about saying goodbye.

That is, until he says, 'Well, I guess this is goodnight.'

I scratch the back of my neck, unsure how to play this. 'Yeah, thanks for the chat and for showing me the secret garden.'

'You're welcome. Maybe we can do it again some time.'

'Sure.' Shit, this suddenly feels like it was a real date. Do I kiss him goodnight? Do I shake his hand like a friend? My brain goes into overdrive, but luckily he takes the lead and leans forwards and gives me a light kiss on my cheek.

'Goodnight ... Eleanor.'

'Goodnight, Eric,' I manage to say with a squeak.

I watch him walk away and then I do a silly little dance on the front step before entering Laura's house and closing the door.

'No boys allowed in the rooms,' says a stern voice.

Laura's sudden presence makes me jump. 'I know,' I say somewhat childishly. Was she spying on us? I'm looking forward to leaving this house even more now, although I will miss Hamilton, who is waiting for me outside my bedroom door.

FRIDAY MORNING ARRIVES and I've barely slept due to the excitement and apprehension of moving to Dawn House. I'm waiting outside the Airbnb at nine as Vera pulls up in her car next to me. I don't have anything on me other than my backpack, so after a quick goodbye to Hamilton, who's watching me from the doorway, I open the door and get in. I said goodbye to Laura over breakfast, during which she was her usual self and asked me far too many questions for my liking. I kept my answers short and then said I needed to pack.

'Morning, Eleanor,' says Vera. I notice she's made an effort to brush her hair this morning and is wearing it down. It reaches just below her shoulders and has some beautiful natural waves through it that plenty of women would kill for.

'Hi. Thanks again for letting me stay with you. I was going to ask about the payment. Is cash, okay? I'm still in the process of setting up a bank account.' A small white lie.

'Yes, that's fine. Does payment every Friday work for you, or would you prefer to pay monthly?'

'Weekly is fine. Here's the first payment.' I hand her five twenty-pound notes, which she takes and stuffs into her jacket pocket.

'Great.' She puts the car in gear and pulls out onto the road.

We sit in silence for a few minutes until we turn onto a narrow road with grass growing in the middle of it. The potholes make me bounce around in my seat.

'Sorry about the state of the road. It gets worse every year. It's only me that uses it really, so I just put up with it.'

I clutch my bag on my lap like it's a life raft as we continue to drive up the severely bumpy road until we finally reach a large wooden gate with a chain and padlock across it, as well as a 'Private Property: Keep Out' sign. Vera gets out without a word, opens it, returns to the car, drives through, closes the gate, locks it up again and drives on. Talk about a severe security system.

'Don't worry about the padlock,' she says. 'It keeps those pesky cold callers out.'

I nod. 'Right.'

'The path to walk to the village starts just there.' She points to the left and I see a narrow, overgrown footpath that looks exceptionally muddy. 'You might want to get yourself some proper boots. I have a pair that should fit you.'

'Thank you. You said the other day that it's about a mile to walk?'

'Yes, not far. You're free to come and go as you please. If you ever need a lift into the village then let me know. Otherwise, I sometimes walk myself when the weather is nice.'

Vera parks the car in the yard next to the large house. My eyes are drawn upwards by the sheer size of the place. My immediate thought is that it looks like a haunted house in a Halloween theme park.

'Wow,' I say, getting out of the car. 'It's big.'

'Yes,' says Vera. 'It used to be much nicer. It's hard to keep up with repairs, though, on a house this size.'

'I'll bet.'

She fishes around in her pocket and hands me a large metal key. 'This is the key to the back door. I only have one key for the front. And this one is the key to your room.' She gives me a smaller silver key, which I take.

'Thanks.'

'Follow me. I'll show you around. I do have a few rules.'

'Of course.'

As I follow Vera up the gravel path to the front door, I catch sight of a black smudge out of the corner of my eye. I turn and see a cat sitting on top of a broken fence, staring straight at me, swishing its tail.

'Oh, you have a cat!'

Vera turns. 'That's Ollie. He's a bit feral. He's not even mine. He just appeared one day and has never really left.'

I walk towards Ollie who hisses at me and then jumps down from the fence and runs off like a black streak of lightning.

'It might take some time for him to trust you.'

I keep my gaze on Ollie as he runs towards a nearby building off to the side of the yard. It looks like a separate garage. He squeezes through the small hole in the door and disappears inside. Perhaps that's where he's made his bed.

Vera is holding the front door open for me, so I jog up to her and step inside. My jaw drops as I take in the enormous entrance hall. Directly in front of me is a vast staircase that swirls up towards the high roof far above. As soon as I close the door behind me, I notice that there isn't much of a difference in temperature between in here and outside.

I pull my jacket tighter.

There's a cricket bat resting on a plinth on the wall next to the front door. It looks like it's engraved and signed. Vera sees me staring at it and says, 'It belonged to my father. His prized possession. Can't bring myself to sell it.'

'He didn't take it with him?'

Vera stares at me. 'I'm sorry?'

I gulp, wondering if maybe I've said something wrong. Am I not meant to know about her parents and brother moving away? 'To Australia, I mean. Sorry, I heard from Eric that they moved there.'

Vera shifts her eyes sideways. 'Yes, well ... my dad wanted to give me something to remember him by.'

I nod and pull my eyes away from the bat.

'What else did he tell you?'

'Who?' I ask.

'That Eric boy.'

'Um, nothing really.'

Vera gives me another stern look but doesn't say anything else. I get the feeling she's a bit guarded about her past. That's okay. I am too.

Several doors lead off from the main hallway, one of which is open, enabling me to see through to the galley kitchen. It's very rustic and there's a large black Aga that looks as if it's hundreds of years old. The kitchen table is made of solid wood. I expect it's very heavy.

'The kitchen,' Vera announces. 'Feel free to buy your own food and keep it in the fridge and cupboards. I can cook your dinner if you like, but breakfast and lunch are on you to sort out. I have ... a few jobs to do in the mornings, which take up a lot of my time.' Vera then points to a door at the far end of the entrance hall. It's plain dark wood, but has a shiny new deadbolt attached with a padlock.

'That's the basement, which is out of bounds,' she says.

'The stairs are broken and there's all sorts of bits and pieces down there that could be dangerous, like ... tools and ... machinery. My dad kept all sorts down there, and I've never cleared the place out.'

My eyes flick over the door as I remember the basement at my parents' house. At least I know I'll never have to run and hide in the basement here. Even if I wanted to, I couldn't, thanks to the deadbolt.

Vera leads me up a flight of stairs, and points to a side bedroom. 'That's my room. All the other rooms in the house are out of bounds too. I had to shut the heating off in most of them to save money. Your attic room is nice and toasty, though, don't worry.'

I manage a small smile, casting a glance at the numerous shut doors along the corridor, all of which have new bolts on. How many bedrooms are there? One thing I've also noticed is that there aren't any homely features such as photographs on the walls, pot plants or any sort of trinkets or decorations – apart from that strange cricket bat. Even the paint on the walls is peeling and plain. The house is devoid of personality. I wonder if it's always been that way or if maybe Vera has had to sell items over the years to keep the place standing. She must really love this house. Maybe it reminds her of her family who abandoned her all those years ago. It's the only piece of them she has left.

There are a hundred questions I want to ask her, but something tells me to take my time before I unleash my inquisitive mind on her.

'Your room is up there. You can use the main bathroom, which is just next to mine. I have an en suite I use most of the time. If you want a bath, then you'll have to tell me in advance as I'll need to go down into the basement to turn on the boost for the hot water otherwise your bath will be very shallow.'

I look up the second set of stairs towards the attic space. They are narrow and dark and there doesn't appear to be a light switch nearby.

'Thanks again, Vera.'

'Dinner is at six.'

'Oh, that's okay. I'm working from noon and won't be back till late.'

'I'll leave a plate in the fridge for you to heat up in the microwave.'

'Thank you.' I don't have the heart to tell her that I'll probably end up eating at the café, as I now feel comfortable taking leftovers from the kitchen staff.

Vera smiles and walks down the stairs, leaving me alone at the foot of the steps leading to the attic. I don't know what the hell people are on about. She's the kindest person I've met in a long time, although I have to admit there is something about her that makes the hair on the back of my neck stand up. All the locked doors for a start.

I can understand she wants her privacy and of course I'll not go venturing into her room, but for most of the rooms to be out of bounds seems a bit harsh. They might be a bit cold, but what's in them that she doesn't want me seeing?

It's clear she's been alone in this house for a long time and that she'd rather not have me here. She's used to doing things her way and on her terms, so I'll do my best to honour her wishes.

I climb the steps into the attic and push open the creaky door at the top. The large space is bare except for a single bed, a wardrobe and a side table. At least it's warmer here than in the rest of the house. However, there is a patch of black damp in the far corner.

I slump down on the bed, which squeaks badly.

I lie still for a few moments, gazing up at the ceiling. And that's when I hear a faint thumping noise emanating throughout the house like a heartbeat.

9

Vera

The idea of Eleanor living under the same roof as me is disconcerting. I'm already nervous and agitated and whenever I think about her being here, my pulse quickens and I feel short of breath. I have no idea how this is going to work, but I'm hoping it won't have to be for too long. Just until my cleaning business picks up over the spring and summer months. I just need a little more time, that's all.

However, I'm not keen on her asking awkward questions, so I hope she learns to keep her mouth shut. How the hell did she know about my story of my parents and brother moving to Australia? Has she been asking questions about me with the locals? The only person I told about my parents moving away was Mr Porter, the butcher. His son, that Eric boy, was only three years old at the time, so his father must have told him about me at some point.

I'll do my best to ensure my new guest is comfortable, but I don't intend to spend any time with her or to get to know her. I'll need to keep her at a distance. I must be careful, especially after what happened last time. I've helped the girl out and that's enough to keep my conscience clear. She's so helpless and lost, like a kitten, but now she's safe as long as she obeys my rules and doesn't ask all those questions, which I could see brewing under the surface as she stared around my house. I'm sure she must be fascinated by the place. Given its foreboding size, there are multitudes of places to explore, but I've told her to keep to certain rooms and not to go traipsing around.

She's a teenager, so it's inevitable she's going to be curious about things and will want to defy the rules. I was the same at her age, but that time of my life seems so long ago now. Back then, I had to grow up fast, especially when my family broke apart so suddenly.

I hated my father, and my mother, so I wasn't sad they died. I wish they'd died sooner, though, then I wouldn't have lost my twin brother in the process. I miss the one-on-one time we used to spend together and his cheeky laugh whenever he would tease me.

Eleanor spends a few hours in her room after I leave her. I really wish I had the money to install a hidden camera outside her room; one of those fancy ones with an app to download on my phone that shows the camera feed, which I could check while I'm out and about. I planned to buy one, but the price was prohibitive, although, to be honest, I very rarely use my phone these days, since I keep getting so many nuisance calls from companies asking for money that I supposedly owe them. I should really change my number, but it's one of those things I haven't gotten around to. As it happens, I don't have that sort of cash to splash on hidden cameras, so for now I'm happy for her to have her privacy, but I do need to keep an eye on her. I need to know where she is within the house. As long as she stays out of the basement. But I'm not too worried about her going down there. Unless she has a metal cutter, there's no way she'll be able to get through the deadbolt I added for extra security. Before, I just used a normal lock and key, but with her in the house I can't be too careful.

Fridays are my rest days. During the summer, I sometimes have a clean or two to do, but not at this time of the year. I usually spend the day bulk cooking dinners for the next week, to save me time. I freeze them and take them out as and when I need them. I do enjoy cooking. It's a welcome distraction, but I can't afford lots of exotic ingredients. I keep to the basic meals; lasagna, fish pie, chickpea curry, chilli con carne and spaghetti bolognese. Then on Saturdays and Sundays, I'll use up any leftovers or maybe treat myself to some sausages from the butcher's in the village. I don't remember the last time I had a proper roast dinner with all the trimmings.

As I knew it would be Eleanor's first night here, I bought enough mince to ensure she could have some of the bolognese I always make on a Friday. I'm not sure if she likes meat, though. I guess she could even be a vegetarian or vegan, but she hasn't said.

The mince is sizzling in the pan on the Aga behind me as I look out across the front garden while I stand at the sink and wash a few plates and cups. It's almost half past five in the evening, and the darkness has settled in already, but there's just enough light to see down to the garage at the bottom of the yard.

My mind drifts to what's located behind the garage. I haven't been back there for a very long time. It's a place I'd rather never go again.

The house is quiet. Eleanor left for work hours ago. I did ask her if she needed me to pick her up from the café, as the path can be tricky to navigate in the dark, but she assured me that she'd be fine and the torch on her phone would be enough to light the way. I reminded her that the front door would be locked and to use the back door instead. She left with a smile and a wave.

I finish the washing up and serve dinner. I put two plates on a tray, add the pasta and top it off with a spoonful of the mince and a sprinkle of grated cheese, then place the third plate on the side to cool, ready for Eleanor when she returns. No doubt she'll be hungry after a long shift.

I take the tray to the basement door and set it on the floor while I unlock the deadbolt using the key that I have around my neck on a thin chain. Once I've flicked the basement lights on, I pick up the tray and descend the stairs carefully. On more than one occasion, I've tripped and tumbled to the bottom, once cracking a rib in the process. There's a dodgy, wobbly stair halfway down that must be trodden on carefully or it can send me off balance, especially if I'm carrying something and can't use the railings for support.

I set the tray on the table next to the large shelving unit, then brace my shoulder against the side of the unit and push. The back of the shelves has a wooden board across it, so the hidden door behind it cannot be seen. The unit slides across the floor with a bit of effort, revealing the door and a small box with a speaker and a button next to it.

I knock three times and wait twenty seconds.

Then press the button as I say, 'Coming in.'

Using the second key on the chain, I unlock the metal door. It emits a loud click. Due to the soundproofing I've installed over the years, the door is heavy and thick with insulated padding. I shove the door open with my shoulder, pick up the tray of food and walk in.

My twin brother sits on the single metal bed in the far corner of the hidden room. His hair is long and matted, his beard scraggly and overgrown. He's wearing an old set of Dad's clothes. It smells pretty ripe when I first walk in, but my senses grow accustomed to it the longer I'm in here.

At six o'clock every evening, I come down here and eat dinner with Kevin. However, I don't go near him anymore, so I eat mine on a chair on the other side of the room from him. He knows what day it is by what I serve.

'Spaghetti bolognese,' I say brightly.

He stares at me with dead, hollow eyes.

PART II

10

25th January 2004

All she could see was Kevin opening and closing his mouth, his eyes as wide as saucers and his arms and hands gesturing wildly. No sound came from his lips, but she nodded along anyway, like watching a silent movie with no subtitles. What was going on? Kevin had killed their parents, but why? What had happened? All Vera could remember were her father's hard fists pummelling into her weak, feverish body, over and over. And the mind-numbing pain. The next thing she remembered was waking up covered in blood in her room, standing up as if not even a moment had passed.

What had happened in between? Why was her memory fuzzy and missing? Was it a defence mechanism her body was putting up, so she didn't have to deal with the trauma of seeing her brother mutilate their parents' bodies, bashing the life from them in front of her eyes?

Kevin stared at her, waving a hand in front of her face, clicking his fingers. Then, as if someone had switched her hearing on, or she'd snapped out of a trance or hypnotic state, his voice came into focus, the volume of it making her jump.

'Vera! Are you listening to me? We have to get rid of their bodies. Now.'

She nodded, her vision still swimming in and out. 'Yes ... yes. We will. I won't let you go to prison. I won't. You're all I have left.' Still kneeling, she threw her arms around his neck, not worrying about the blood and rain that soaked into her nightdress. The thought of losing Kevin filled her with so much terror she couldn't stand it. Being alone in this world was something she never wanted to experience. Ever.

Kevin squeezed her tight. 'We'll be okay, Vera.'

'What happened?'

'You still don't remember?'

'I remember Dad hitting me. I must have blacked out. The next thing I remember is waking up alone in my room covered in blood. I followed the blood smears down the stairs and then saw you at the door holding the bat.'

Kevin's eyes drifted to the floor. 'He wouldn't stop hitting you. I thought he was going to kill you. I was so scared. You told me to run.'

Vera sniffed loudly and wiped her eyes with the damp cuff of her nightdress, leaving a smear of blood on her cheek. 'It's okay. I don't blame you. I'd have done the same thing to protect you.'

Kevin reached out his hand and gently wiped the smear of blood off her cheek using his finger. He couldn't quite meet her gaze. 'We have to bury them. The ground will be soaked and easier to dig. I've dragged them outside behind the garage. If we get the police involved, then ... I don't know what will happen, but I can't let them come and separate us. We must stick together.'

Vera nodded, taking Kevin's hand as he stood up. He pulled her to her feet. She stumbled sideways, feeling as if the whole world had just titled on an axis. Her head pounded as if a tiny drummer was inside, beating against her skull. She was freezing, yet felt as if she were on fire. The fever was raging through her body, fighting for control, but she couldn't let it take her. Not yet. She had to make sure her brother was safe. She'd need to hide him and take care of him while things blew over. Their parents' absence would be noticed at some point. Questions would be asked. She couldn't allow Kevin to be questioned by the police because she knew what would happen.

He'd surely confess if pushed too far for fear of Vera taking the blame. She couldn't let him do that. He'd saved her life, and now she was determined to save his.

Vera slipped her bare feet into her dark green Wellington boots, grimacing as they squelched inside; her feet were covered in blood. Next, she grabbed her father's waterproof jacket from the peg by the door, shrugging into it even though the action seemed pointless considering she was already drenched in sweat and blood. It was far too big, but she zipped it up and pulled up the hood before following Kevin into the yard. He handed her a torch.

The garage light was on, illuminating the surrounding area, but around the back where Kevin led Vera was cast in shadows, the light not quite reaching all the way around. It was probably for the best. The nearest neighbour was almost half a mile away across the fields and a river, but they couldn't be too careful. It was unlikely anyone would be out walking this early in the morning, but Vera had known the local farmers to be awake at this time before, especially during a storm, checking for damage or flooding.

Kevin was right. The ground was sodden, and no sooner had she arrived at the scene, her feet slid out from under her and she landed on her bottom in the mud. Kevin pulled her to her feet again, struggling to gain balance himself.

'You okay?' he asked.

'Ask me again when this is all over,' she replied. 'Where are they?'

Kevin pointed to the left of where they were standing. Vera shone her torch and had to stifle a scream with both her hands when she saw the bloody mass of two bodies. Her eyes couldn't work out where one body began, and another ended. Kevin had piled them on top of each other, but she saw to her horror that one of them was missing a head.

She stepped closer. No, it had a head, but it was smashed to a pulp. The face and skull of her father wasn't recognisable. Teeth, hair, blood and bone looked as if they had been pulverised in a blender and then dumped on the ground in a pile. Her mother's face was in better shape, but her jaw was badly broken, connected to her skull by only skin and muscle.

Vera lurched to the side and vomited. Her brother had done that. He hadn't just stopped them with a blow to the head. He'd unleashed hell on them, beating them to a bloody pulp.

The rain still beat down relentlessly. She tore her eyes away from the bodies and watched her brother as he sliced into the soft soil with a spade. He hadn't bothered with a coat of any sort. His wet shirt now clung to his torso. His eyes were focused and every movement of his body was strong and aggressive, determined.

She offered to help, but he declined, saying she wasn't strong enough, so she leaned against the garage wall and watched while her brother dug a large hole. She did ask halfway through if she should go back to the house to start cleaning up, but Kevin said he wanted her to stay close so he could keep an eye on her. What did he mean by that?

When the hole was finally big enough, he threw the spade to the side and slumped down on the ground, exhausted.

But now the hole was filling up with water, and fast.

Vera helped him grab their mother first and together they dragged her into the watery grave. Next, they moved their father. Kevin had done a decent job with the depth of the hole. They pulled him to the edge, then Kevin kicked him, and he half slid, half fell in, landing with a sickening splash.

Vera couldn't tear her eyes away from the gruesome sight, so she didn't realise how close to the edge she was. The sodden ground simply gave way, plummeting her to the bottom, where she landed on top of the pulpy mass that was her father and mother. She shrieked, trying desperately to escape, but everything was so wet and slippery that she couldn't get any kind of grip.

'Stop fighting, Vera. Just calm down,' shouted Kevin. Vera stopped and remained still, forcing herself to focus on her breathing all the while surrounded by death. 'Take the end of the spade!'

Vera opened her eyes and saw the handle of the spade.

She grabbed it and, with an almighty effort, Kevin pulled her up the side, out of the filthy, hellish grave.

'Go back inside the house,' he said. 'Start cleaning up. I'll be with you in a moment.'

She didn't want to leave him. She couldn't, but he insisted.

Vera walked slowly back to the house and stood in the entrance hall, dripping muddy water all over the floor. It wasn't over yet. Once they'd cleaned up, she'd have to hide Kevin for a while. And she'd have to lie low too. How long would it take before someone knocked on the door? Maybe she could pretend that her parents and brother had moved away. Maybe Australia? Somewhere so far away that it was unlikely they'd ever return or be heard from again.

But then what?

Vera's mind was a muddle of questions, worries and fear. She needed to make a decision. And she needed to make it now.

11

Elle

Over the next two days, I hardly see Vera. We're like passing ships in the night. She tends to go to bed early, around nine, whereas I don't get back from my late shifts until gone ten. The light is still on in her bedroom, though. I can see it escaping through the cracks around the door as I pass it on my way to my attic room. True to her word, she leaves me dinner in the fridge every evening, which I eat, foregoing the leftovers at the café so I can have a homecooked meal instead. I only have late shifts at the weekend and on Thursdays, so tonight I'll be back at dinnertime to eat with Vera.

On Monday morning, I'm not due at work until one in the afternoon, so I decide to explore the house and grounds as much as I can, as I haven't been able to do that since I've been here thanks to the weekends being extra busy at work.

However, my plan to explore the house is short-lived because the only rooms I can enter are the kitchen and the living room. As Vera said, all the bedrooms are locked, as is the dining room and a couple of other rooms on the ground floor. The room that intrigues me the most is the basement for no other reason than I used to like my old basement in my house and I'm curious as to what the layout is like.

I hang around the door and give the handle a little shake, but the deadbolt holds fast.

'What are you doing?'

I jump and spin around to find Vera standing in the doorway with her arms folded, glaring at me.

'I'm sorry ... I didn't mean ...'

'The basement is out of bounds.'

'Right. Sorry.' I feel awful. She gave me rules to follow and I'm here trying to break them out of nothing other than curiosity. 'I was thinking of going for a walk,' I say, hoping a change of subject will draw her attention away from the fact I was fiddling with the basement door. The weather has dried up and the sun is shining for what seems like the first time this winter.

Vera looks at me without blinking for almost ten seconds. Is she trying to scare me? Because she's doing a damn good job if that's her intention. What if she kicks me out for breaking her rules?

'There's a river at the bottom of the yard,' she says. 'And a footpath alongside it.'

I nod. 'Thanks. Um ... I'll be back about five. I only have a short shift today.'

Vera's eyes widen briefly. 'It's fish pie for dinner on a Monday.'

'I'll be back in time to eat with you.'

'Don't worry if you're a bit late,' she says quickly.

I frown, slightly confused as to why she appears so nervous. Does she not want me to come for dinner and eat with her? I suppose having lived here alone for two decades, she's not used to eating with anyone. Maybe I can help her adjust to socialising again.

'See you later,' I say.

I can feel her eyes on the back of my head as I walk out the door and down the path towards the yard. I walk past the garage and am about to follow the natural path down to the river when something stops me in my tracks.

Ollie is digging in the earth at the back of the garage. He looks up when he notices me, opens his mouth and lets out a loud meow, then returns to digging his hole. Maybe he's about to go to the toilet. But he keeps on digging with such persistence it's like he's searching for buried treasure.

I leave Ollie to his digging and walk to the river.

I really need to invest in some decent footwear and new clothes. I make a mental note to ask Vera where the nearest clothes shop is tonight. I doubt there's one in the village, not one suitable to my taste anyway, but I bet there's a charity shop. I would order stuff online, but I'm trying to keep my digital footprint as low as possible, so I have stopped using my online shopping accounts and email address.

I walk along the river path for thirty minutes, enjoying the scenery and the peace and quiet. I don't see another living soul, apart from birds and a rabbit which darts across the path in front of me, making me jump out of my skin. After thirty minutes, I turn and walk the same way back to the house. I'd rather not get lost trying to find a different path back. The clean, fresh air invigorates my body and by the time I reach the garage again my legs ache slightly from the exertion, but in a good way. After being on my feet all day at the café for over a week now, my legs are getting stronger and more used to the intensity of the work.

Ollie is nowhere to be seen. I assume he's off somewhere else hunting for food or maybe curled up having a nap. I head to the side of the garage and peer through the dirty window. There isn't a lot inside, from what I can see, except for an old lawn mower that's not been used in years, an array of shovels, spades, gardening equipment and a couple of metal buckets covered in rust. As I move away from the wall, a dark stain catches my eye. It's smeared next to the window frame.

'Did you have a nice walk?'

My body leaps away from the window and my hand goes straight to my heart to steady it. Vera has a knack for sneaking up on me.

'Yes, I did,' I say, panting slightly. 'I saw Ollie here earlier, digging around in the dirt.'

Vera's eyes scan the surrounding area. 'That cat is always digging up my garden, using it as a toilet.'

'I'd better get ready for work,' I say.

'See you for dinner,' says Vera.

'At six,' I say brightly.

She narrows her eyes at me. 'Yes. Six.'

'Oh, I was going to ask … Is there a shop where I can buy new clothes somewhere around here? I only brought a couple of spare sets with me, and please can I do some washing?'

Vera nods. 'Yes, use the washing machine whenever you need to, but keep it on the short cycle and cold wash. And there's a clothes shop in the next town over. How come you brought so little with you?'

I feel as though I'm entering dangerous territory. I don't want her asking too many questions about where I came from. It almost feels like we're in a stalemate. If I stop snooping around, then she'll not ask questions about where I came from and why I'm really here.

'I felt like starting afresh,' I say with a casual shrug. 'Maybe you could come with me?'

Vera frowns. 'Come with you where?'

'Clothes shopping.'

'Why?'

Shit. I don't want to let on that I think her dress sense is dire (which it is), or that she could do with a makeover. 'Just ... maybe it's time you had a fresh start too.' I hold my breath; I'm afraid I've taken it too far. Vera stares at me.

'Let me know when you want to go. I'll drive you,' she says.

I let out my breath. 'Thank you.'

WHEN I ARRIVE at work that afternoon, Eric is at the counter ordering his usual coffees for himself and his dad. Double shot latte and a cappuccino with oat milk, extra-large. Seeing him again sends flutters of excitement through my body and turns my mouth dry. He sees me and his whole face beams into a smile and he waves. I wave back as I approach.

'Hi,' I say, unable to say much else because all I can think is how good his hair looks.

'Hey, how are you settling in at Vera's?'

'Oh, um, good, I guess. We don't see much of each other, to be honest,' I say with a casual shrug.

Carl is serving him behind the counter. He turns and

hands Eric his drinks and then looks at me. 'You're staying at Vera's now?'

'Yeah, in her attic room.'

'What's her house like?' asks Eric. 'As kids we were always told to stay away from her place.'

'Um ... it's ... big and a bit run-down, but nice.'

Carl gives me a hard look. 'Just be careful, yeah? Vera's a bit of an odd one.'

Eric nods in response, but then he must notice the confusion in my face because he adds, 'But don't worry. I'm sure all the stories about her aren't true.'

'What stories?'

Eric shakes his head. 'Never mind. Forget I brought it up.' He turns to Carl. 'Cheers for the coffees, Carl.' Carl gives him a salute and then starts cleaning the counters. 'So, you doing anything later. Fancy hanging out again?'

'Oh, um, actually, I told Vera I'd eat dinner with her tonight.'

His face falls, but he covers it up quickly. 'No problem. I'll see you around then, yeah?'

'Yeah, totally.' I watch him leave, feeling a bit guilty about blowing him off like that. I could have given him my number, but the less people who have that the better. Besides, I haven't used my phone since being here. I've no need for it.

I head into the back to grab my apron, but while I'm tying it around my waist, the radio alerts me to the start of the news.

'Elle Walter, a Gloucester-based seventeen-year-old has been reported missing by her parents. She disappeared on twenty-fourth of January and hasn't been seen since. Police are currently scouring CCTV at train and bus stations. Residents in the surrounding area are advised to be on the lookout for her. She has long black hair, is five-foot-five and of a slender build.'

My stomach does a somersault and all the oxygen whooshes from the room, leaving me breathless.

'Bloody hell, are you okay, Eleanor? You look even paler than usual,' says Stacey.

I lunge forward and switch off the radio. 'Yes, I'm fine. Thanks. Just ... a dizzy spell.'

'Have you eaten?'

'Yes. Honestly, I'm fine.'

It takes almost an hour before my heart rate returns to a normal rhythm, and the swirling vortex of anxiety builds in my stomach all day. Why would my parents bother to look for me? Do they really care about my wellbeing, or do they just want the media attention? Also, I can't help but notice, it's taken them almost a week to report me missing, unless they did report it straight away and it hasn't been announced to the media until now. It's difficult to tell, but I can't dwell on it too much, or bring attention to the news. It won't take people long to put two and two together.

I decide to buy some hair dye and bleach from the corner shop on my way home. Not a lot will cover black, but even if I can make it slightly lighter, it will help. Maybe I'll pick up some dye for Vera too, and we can have a hair dye party.

Or maybe not.

12

Vera

Tonight is fish pie for dinner. It's creeping closer to six o'clock and almost time for me to take Kevin his dinner. We've had the same routine for nearly twenty years. Dinner is at six. Always. I usually eat it with him too, and we watch the six o'clock news, followed by a soap opera. I set up the television for him ten years ago, running the cable from upstairs, because I was beginning to worry about his sanity. I don't allow him to watch it when I'm not there, though. A few years ago, I had Netflix set up, but I couldn't justify the cost after a while, since I rarely watch television anyway, so I cancelled it.

But now I've run into a big problem. Eleanor is due back from work at any moment, so there's no way I can give Kevin his dinner on time. I've been able to do it for the past few days because she's worked late, but now I'm going to have to rethink my routine. I can't dish up his dinner and leave it on the side because Eleanor will see it and wonder who the extra plate is for.

Maybe I can quickly take him his food and leave him to eat it himself, or ...

The back door swings open and Eleanor enters. 'Hi, Vera,' she says.

'Just in time,' I say brightly, even though I'm seething inside. Kevin will have to wait tonight. He won't be happy about it, and he can't know why his routine has changed. If he finds out there's someone living in this house, he will make more noise. The soundproofing is already not working as well as it once did, and I can't figure out why. Often, I hear banging and shouts, even if they are muffled. There must be a hole in the padding somewhere, but I've done a check of the room's interior and it all looks in place. I can't afford to repair it. I installed it myself, a year after I first put him down there. He spent a lot of time shouting for help. Not that anyone could hear him since our house is so remote, but his shouts kept me awake at night, so I had to block out the noise somehow.

'It smells wonderful,' says Eleanor as she shrugs out of her jacket and hangs it on the peg by the door.

'What's in the bag?' I ask. I turn to the oven and remove the pie.

'Hair dye,' she replies.

'Oh? Your hair looks lovely as it is.'

'Thanks, but I was thinking of going lighter. I have some bleach. I was wondering if you could help me apply it tonight.'

'Uh ... yes. I don't see why not.'

'I hope you don't mind, but I bought some dye for you too.'

'You did? You didn't have to do that, Eleanor.'

'You don't have to use it. I just thought ...'

'I appreciate what you're trying to do, but there's no need. I don't have time to treat myself to things like that.'

'Everyone deserves to be pampered once in a while.'

'I don't.'

Eleanor places the bag on the side. 'Well, I think you do.'

I almost burst into tears. No one has cared enough to do anything nice for me in the past twenty years. The last person who did something with my happiness in mind is now locked in my basement. I don't deserve this special treatment, nor do I want it. Her concern and kindness are dangerous. I should push her away, kick her out of this house and come up with another plan to earn more money, but something stops me; the yearning to be close to another person.

Technically, I've not been living alone all these years, but I have been keeping a secret, which has stopped me from forming any sort of outside relationship, be it friendship or otherwise, and it has slowly eaten away at what was left of my soul. Kevin's captivity has forced me to hide myself away from others, so despite him still being a part of my life, he's destroyed it.

I've always yearned to be a mother and to have a daughter. Ever since I was a little girl, I've wanted a child of my own to raise, nurture and look after. I believe I'd be a wonderful parent. I'd ensure I didn't treat my child the way my parents treated me. I've been denied that opportunity by having to look after Kevin and protect his safety. He's family, and I love him, so it was an easy choice to make at the time, but as the years have passed, I've grown to resent him and now realise how debilitating his care is to my own life.

'Let's do it,' I say. 'But let's eat first.'

IT'S GONE HALF past nine by the time Eleanor and I finish dying each other's hair. I had to use a lot of bleach on Eleanor's black hair to lighten it, but now she's sporting a light brown/dark blonde colour, which softens her pale skin. My hair is now chocolate brown and there's not a sign of my grey strands. Eleanor even gave it a trim, expertly cutting off the split ends and tidying up the back. It's never looked this shiny and healthy before, and I barely recognise myself.

While we did our hair, we watched a game show. It was mainly just on in the background to cover up any noise coming from the basement. I don't say a lot, but Eleanor reveals a few snippets of information about where she grew up in Bath and her favourite classes at school. She wants to be a fashion designer and has plans to save up to attend university in a couple of years.

I don't press her for details regarding her parents, as it's not hard to figure out that they're a sore topic of conversation, much like my own.

Eleanor bids me goodnight once the game show finishes, and I watch her walk up the stairs to her room. I head into the kitchen and dish out a plate of fish pie, which is now cold. I heat it up in the microwave for two minutes while I set out the tray and a drink of water.

Carefully, I descend the basement stairs, slide the shelves aside, unlock the door and enter. Kevin sits on his bed, his ankles bound by the metal cuffs. He looks up at me and I see the confusion in his eyes.

'What time do you call this?'

There's no clock in this room, but Kevin is an expert at figuring out the time without one. I have no idea how he does it. 'It's a little after six,' I say. 'It took longer to cook than I thought.'

'Don't lie to me, Vera. It must be gone nine by now. Why are you three hours late bringing my dinner? You've never been late before. What's going on?'

I step to the side and place the tray on the trolley, pushing it towards him with a long pole that's propped in the corner. Over the years, I've had to adapt my treatment of Kevin. He's lashed out at me on more than one occasion, knocked the tray out of my hands and attempted to use the cutlery as a weapon. Now, I keep my distance and don't allow him close enough to touch me. It's too risky. I know he doesn't mean to hurt me. He's like a trapped animal. All he wants is to escape, but it's far too dangerous for him in the outside world. It's safer for him here. It's safer for everyone.

'Nothing is going on. I had a late cleaning job, that's all.'

'Liar.'

'I'm not lying, Kevin. Now, do you want your dinner or not?'

Kevin glares at me and then slowly reaches out for the trolley and pulls it closer. He begins to eat, taking small bites, savouring every mouthful.

'Aren't you going to put the television on?' he asks, nodding towards the locked cabinet in the far corner. Sometimes I think about taking it away, but it's all he has in the way of entertainment.

'I'm tired. I'm going to bed,' I say.

Kevin scoffs. 'Whatever.' Then he looks at me again and tilts his head. 'What have you done to your hair?'

'I dyed it and had it trimmed.'

'Why?'

'Because I felt like it.'

Another scoff. 'You've never done anything like this in twenty years. Why now?'

I touch my bouncy hair. 'We're in our mid-thirties, Kevin. I'm getting grey hair.'

'Join the club. How about giving me a trim? My hair and beard smell like a sewer.'

'I'd rather not, especially after the last time I tried.'

'You could always drug me. That's what you like to do sometimes, isn't it? Who was at the door the other day?' I turn to leave, not willing to start that topic of conversation. 'Vera, wait!'

I don't listen. I slam and lock the door.

How had Kevin heard the doorbell when the electrician visited? Granted, the soundproofing isn't one hundred per cent guaranteed. I don't drug him often, but sometimes I need to, such as when I need to bathe him, but it's becoming more and more difficult to do. It's been several months since I've been able to give him a bath. Now, I just give him a bucket of soapy water and a sponge and let him do it himself. But he doesn't do it properly. It's almost like he's trying to punish me by not washing himself, like he's blaming me for his poor health and living conditions. I give him plenty of food and water, multivitamins, the ability to wash himself and some entertainment. It's as good as what prisoners get in real prisons, although they get to go outside for exercise. Kevin hasn't seen daylight or breathed fresh air in two decades.

There have been too many close calls over the years. He's strong and determined to escape, his desire growing with each day. Now, there's someone in this house who could ruin everything. I need to keep him compliant, so that sprinkling of powered sleeping tablets in his food tonight should be enough to keep him sedated.

I don't have any other choice. I have to protect him, like he protected me all those years ago. He may hate me for what I've done, but I've done it for his own good. I wish he'd understand that rather than blame me.

I go upstairs to my room, but before I can turn in for the night, I have some packing envelopes and boxes to do; my small side job that keeps a few more quid coming in. I hate doing it, but I can't afford not to. All I want to do is sleep, but I force my eyes to stay open while I pack and sort the envelopes and boxes that are due to be sent out tomorrow. The job is very repetitive, and I find myself going through the motions without really putting much thought into it. It's gone midnight by the time I finish and crawl into bed, falling asleep almost as soon as my head hits the pillow.

13

Elle

As I get ready for bed, I can't help but feel Vera and I have turned a corner in our relationship. Tonight was fun, and even though I couldn't share all the details about my life before I came here, it was nice to speak to someone who listened and cared about what I was saying. She seemed to hang on my every word.

She didn't share a lot of her own background, but I could feel her barriers slowly coming down. It would be nice to have a friend, even though she's about twenty years older than me. She seems old enough to be my mum, but there's something about her that makes me feel safe. Sort of like a big sister and a mum rolled into one, even if she is a little eccentric.

I wonder if she's ever had children or wanted them. Maybe she had them early on in life and now they're grown up, although I doubt it. According to the locals, she's been living alone in this house for twenty years. She must miss her brother and parents. I wanted to ask her about them earlier, but there will be time for that later.

I stand in front of the small mirror in the bathroom and admire my lighter hair. Vera said it suited me, and I have to agree. I will miss my black hair. I just hope it's not too late. Will Stacey and Carl be suspicious that I've dyed my hair, or will they not care enough to put two and two together? Hopefully, it will keep me hidden under the radar for a while longer until my parents give up their search for me. It still baffles me that they've made any effort to find me.

I WAKE up and head downstairs at six. I'm on the early shift at work. I put some brown bread into the toaster and flick the kettle on to make myself a flask of tea to drink on my walk into the village. I'm not sure where Vera is. She's awake and up because I heard her take a shower this morning. I remember her saying she has chores to do in the mornings, but I still don't know what they are exactly. As far as I know, she doesn't have any animals to feed and look after, apart from Ollie. Maybe it has something to do with her cleaning or packing business. She said she has another job packing boxes and stuffing envelopes from home to earn extra money. I must remember to ask her about that.

While I wait for the kettle to boil, I stare out the window above the sink and out onto the yard. I watch as two small birds land on the windowsill and start pecking at the dirt embedded in the cracks. The closer I look at this house, the more I realise how much of a state it's in. It must have been glorious two decades ago. It's such a shame it's in this sorry state now. I can understand Vera's reluctance to leave – up to a point. It was the last place she saw her family. Why did they move away and leave her? The story is so strange and fascinating. Maybe I can help her. Maybe I can try and find out where they moved to and reunite them. Would she think that was overstepping the mark? Perhaps it is.

A scraping noise makes me turn and look over my shoulder. Someone is dragging something heavy across a hard floor. I know because it's roughly the same sound the shelving unit used to make as I pulled it away from the wall back in my old house.

I walk into the hallway and stop short when I see the basement door is ajar. Vera's down in the basement moving something.

I reach out to pull the door open when Vera appears. I leap back in fright.

'What are you doing?' she asks, a harsh note to her voice.

'Sorry, I was about to come down and help you with whatever it is you were moving.'

'I wasn't moving anything. Stay out of the basement.' She slams the door shut and bolts it before stomping past me into the kitchen.

Our fragile relationship appears to have been broken overnight. I'm only trying to help her, but she insists on pushing me away.

I pour hot water into the flask and butter my toast. Vera is doing a load of laundry. It looks as if she washes all the towels from the Airbnbs she cleans.

'I'm sorry, Vera. I really am.'

She lets out a long sigh. 'Eleanor, I'm only keeping you out of the basement for your protection. The stairs are very wonky and if you were to trip and fall ... I care about you,

Eleanor. I don't want you to get hurt. Also, if you were to go down there and the door swung shut, you'd be locked inside until I came to let you out. It can't be opened from the inside. I've tried fixing the lock, but I can't.'

I nod my understanding. 'Can I ask you a question?'

'It's not about the basement, is it?'

I smile. 'No. You mentioned you had another job. The packing one? I'd be happy to help you with it. You don't even need to pay me, since you're letting me live here.'

Vera's eyes widen. 'I'd have to pay you something, Eleanor. But thank you; with two people doing the work, we'd get more done. I was planning on doing some more this afternoon.'

'I finish work at four.'

'Then I'll see you at around half four. I do the packing in my bedroom. Please knock before you come in.'

'I will. Thanks. See you later.'

'Have a good day, Eleanor.'

I ARRIVE at work with a smile on my face, which gets even bigger when I see Eric waiting for me outside the café. When he sees me, he raises his hand and waves enthusiastically.

'Hey, Eleanor. I'm glad I caught you. Oh wow, great hair. What prompted that?'

I instinctively tuck a stray strand behind my left ear. 'Just fancied a change.'

'It suits you.'

'Thanks! Did you want to talk to me about something?'

'Um, yeah ... I wanted to ask how you're getting on living with Vera.'

Why is he so interested in Vera? 'Really good. We're becoming friends.'

Eric raises his eyebrows. 'Nice. Listen, are you free tonight? Can I take you out for a drink?'

I freeze as a thousand questions buzz through my mind. Does he mean a drink as friends or a proper date? Is this a second date? And by drink does he mean an alcoholic drink or a Coke?

'Sorry, but I can't tonight. I have plans.'

'Tomorrow?'

'Um, sure. Tomorrow sounds good.' If he does mean an alcoholic drink, then I'll make something up. He doesn't need to know I'm underage and that I don't drink. 'I finish work at six.'

'I'll come and meet you.'

'Okay, see you then.'

'Bye, Eleanor. Oh ... your new hair colour really does suit you.'

A flicker of a smile brushes my lips, but inside my stomach clenches in panic as a random thought enters my head. If the news is on the radio, then it sure as hell will be online and there will be a photo of me out there for the world to see. Does he already know who I am and that's why he mentioned my hair more than once? Am I in danger of being found out? I'd rather die than go back to my parents' house.

I tell myself to calm down and stop being so quick to judge. I'm sure he just said it as a compliment. I tell myself that I'm safe here, as long as I stay vigilant and don't share too much information with people.

14

25th January 2004

Vera shook so violently as she sat and waited for Kevin that it looked like she was having a seizure. She couldn't think about anything other than hiding her brother, just for a little while. But where was the best place? Perhaps the attic. It used to be their old playroom, but they hadn't been up there in years, not since they'd become teenagers and stopped playing together.

Then she remembered the cold storage room in the basement.

Vera hobbled along the hallway. When she'd first fallen down the stairs, she hadn't realised just how hard she'd landed. Now, her left leg was throbbing. She pulled open the door to the basement and crept down the stairs. She remembered too late about the wonky step and swore loudly as she tipped over sideways against the railing. Her dad had always meant to fix that step. She stumbled to the bottom, swearing as her leg exploded in pain. Catching her breath, she flicked on the lights. The whole basement lit up, revealing a bare yet tidy area, complete with the boiler, water tank and electric meter all together in the nearest corner to the stairs.

But there was also a small room leading off from the main basement.

It was an old cold storage room and sometimes her father would shove them both inside as a punishment. It couldn't be opened from the inside and the door was lockable. If she gave him plenty of blankets, then he'd survive perfectly well in there for a few weeks. It was perfect. She could even hide the door if she needed to, in case the police came, by pulling a shelving unit in front of it and boarding up the back.

'Vera?' Kevin's voice echoed above her. 'Where are you?'

'Down here,' she called out. Thundering footsteps sounded as he ran down the stairs. 'Watch out!'

She was too late again. Kevin's left foot caught on the wonky step, and he tumbled headfirst, landing with a sickening thud at the bottom of the stairs.

Vera didn't move a muscle.

He was dead. She'd killed him by just being down here, by forgetting about that damn step.

Vera let out a garbled cry as she sank to the floor, her hands covering her face. What had she done? It was all her fault. It was ...

'Urrrgg ...'

'Kevin?' Vera rushed to his side. 'You're alive?'

'That fucking step,' he muttered.

'Are you okay?'

'My head ...' Kevin sat up and touched the back of his

head. His fingers came away covered in blood, but it was difficult to know if it belonged to him or their parents. 'I'm okay ... I think. What the hell are you doing down here? I thought you were going to start cleaning up.'

'I was ... I will ... but I have an idea.'

'Which is?'

'I'm the oldest. I need to keep you safe. You saved my life and now I'm going to do the same for you.'

Kevin rolled into a sitting position. 'What are you talking about?'

'The cold storage room.'

'What about it?'

'You can hide out in there while everything blows over. I can tell everyone that you and our parents moved away. No one will ever know what happened. Once enough time has passed, maybe a few weeks, we can leave this house and start our lives somewhere else.'

Kevin shook his head. 'That makes no sense, Vera. No one is going to believe that we moved away and left you here by yourself.'

'They might. I'll keep quiet. I'll keep myself to myself. People around here didn't even like Mum and Dad. They will be relieved that they are gone. If the police or anyone turn up and start asking questions, then you're in danger. No matter how much we clean, we won't be able to get rid of all the evidence, all the bloodstains. Trust me. Hide out in the room for a while. I'll sort everything out.'

'I'm not letting you deal with this by yourself. We're in this together, remember?'

Vera hung her head, defeated. There was no changing his mind. Kevin was as stubborn as they came. 'Fine, you win.'

'Thank you. Now, come and help me clean upstairs. You're good at cleaning.'

'Sexist much?'

Kevin smirked. 'Let's go.'

'Are you sure your head is okay?'

'I'll be fine.'

Vera followed him up the stairs and fetched a bucket and mop from the hallway cupboard while Kevin collected bleach and cloths. They split up; Kevin took downstairs, Vera went upstairs. As she knelt on the floor and mopped up the blood as best she could, she noticed something glinting in the dark underneath her bed.

Vera reached forwards and grabbed the item. It was the silver bracelet Kevin had given her; the reason why her father had attacked her and the reason why both her parents were now dead and buried behind the garage. It was supposed to have been a kind gesture from her twin brother on their birthday, but now it was a symbol of death. She tried to attach it back around her wrist, vowing to never remove it, but the clasp was broken. Her father must have grabbed it and snapped it during his attack.

Vera closed her eyes, trying to remember, but nothing was coming to her. There was nothing but haziness where the memory should be. As she looked around the room, she realised something: this was where Kevin had killed her father, but what about their mother? Kevin said that she had joined in the attack, and he'd had to kill her too, but it didn't make sense.

Their mother had never laid a hand on them before. Granted, she'd stood by and watched as their father had hit them, but she'd never done it herself. Unless she'd attacked Kevin to try and stop him from killing their father.

Another thing that didn't make sense was where the bat had come from. It was usually on a plinth in the hallway downstairs, so had Kevin run downstairs, grabbed the bat, headed back upstairs and then attacked their father, all while their father had been hitting Vera?

Had he set out to kill him or was it an accident?

Something wasn't right. The chain of events didn't add up to Kevin's story. He was lying, which meant he was dangerous. Had he had a mental breakdown? Could he attack someone else in the future? One thing was certain: Kevin couldn't be trusted. She needed to keep him away from other people until she could figure out what to do.

15

Vera

Last night was a complete disaster. Kevin now knows something is wrong. He could practically smell the lies wafting from my pores. I can't tell him about Eleanor living in the house. I love my brother so much, more than anything, but he's such a burden on my life, and he's dangerous. Spending time with Eleanor has given me back a purpose, a spark of humanity that I've been missing all these years. Human beings need contact with other human beings to survive, or they become shells of their former selves, which is exactly what's happened to Kevin. He's not the same person who went into the room twenty years ago. Back then, he understood why he had to stay hidden, but now he'd do anything to escape. I can't let him. Lives are at stake. Not just his. I wouldn't put it past him that he'd kill me or Eleanor if he had the chance.

Seven years ago, that almost happened. Back then, he'd allow me near him to trim his hair and shave his beard. I had to keep the chains on him, though, because I had to leave the door open to the hidden room. At the time I hadn't figured out a way to keep it closed and locked that would still enable me to leave. That's when I installed the small lock with the key. I was using a pair of scissors to cut his hair when he suddenly overpowered me, grabbed the scissors, held them to my throat.

'Unlock my cuffs!' he'd screamed in my ear. His whole body was shaking violently. I knew he didn't want to hurt me. I calmly told him that it wasn't safe for him to be set free. The police were still looking for him.

'It's been thirteen years. How could they still be looking for me?' he'd demanded.

'I'm trying to protect you,' I told him.

He began to cry, as he dug the tip of the scissors deeper into my skin, drawing blood. I remained calm, took a deep breath, then elbowed him in the stomach, grabbed the scissors off him and ran towards the door.

'You've just lost your bathing privileges,' I said as I slammed the door shut. I left him in there with no food or water for two days. He needed to know how serious I was.

It was then I decided he needed something to keep him sane, so I allowed him to read one book per week, and I set up the television. I always ensured I was with him when we watched television, but he didn't talk to me for almost a year after that incident. I thought he might have been irreversibly damaged at this point, but he eventually started talking again. Even so, I've never touched him or been within four feet of him since.

· · ·

THAT EVENING, before Eleanor returns from work, I give Kevin his dinner two hours early, so I don't have to take it to him later. He stares at me as I push the food trolley towards him.

'I don't like this,' he says, staring blankly at the dinner plate. I'm forced to feed him on a plastic plate now in case he decides to smash it and use the shards to hurt himself.

'It's chickpea curry. It's what I cook every single week.'

'No, I meant I don't like this change in routine. Why are you doing this?'

'I have other things to do now.'

'Like what?'

I stare at my brother for a moment. He smells ripe and clearly hasn't been washing himself properly with the hot soapy water and flannel I provide him with. I have given him some clean clothes, which once belonged to our father, but he refuses to wear them. He's been wearing the same thing for almost four years, and I don't know how I'm supposed to keep him clean and healthy if he refuses to use the products I provide.

'Kevin, we need to talk about your cleanliness situation. It smells like something has died in here.'

'Something has,' he says slowly as he picks up the plastic spoon. 'My soul.'

'You're so dramatic.'

He raises his eyes to meet mine. 'I'm dramatic?' Then he laughs and the sound sends shivers up and down my spine. It's not a joyous laugh. It's a laugh that could curdle milk, full of hatred and venom. 'You think I'm the crazy one, Vera? You've kept your twin brother locked in a room for two decades. You're one crazy bitch.'

'To keep you safe,' I snap back. 'Everything I've ever done

has been for your safety and benefit. Do you want to go to prison, Kevin?'

'I'm in prison,' he snaps. 'What I want is a chance at a new life. That's what you promised me, Vera.'

'I can't let you go, Kevin. We've been over this. You're too dangerous. You're reckless. You murdered our parents. You bashed their brains in with a cricket bat. I can't risk you hurting anyone else.'

Kevin laughs again, shaking his head. 'That's where you're wrong. I'm not the dangerous one.'

'I've never hurt you. Ever.'

'Oh, fuck off,' he mutters, lowering his head to his food.

I exit the room and lock the door, returning the shelving unit in front of it. He's wrong. I know he'll do anything to escape. He'll say anything. Maybe he'd be better off dead. At least then I'd be free from him. I'm just as much of a prisoner as he is. He has no idea the sacrifices I've made for him, to keep him safe, to keep others safe. But I can't kill him. He's my brother and I love him. Without him, I'd have no one.

Or would I? I have Eleanor now, who's beginning to feel more like a friend or daughter to me every day. I can't trust her yet, but maybe one day I will.

I'VE GOT through packing a hundred envelopes and fifteen boxes by the time I hear the back door open. I used to let Kevin do this job. It's easy and kept him occupied, but I had to keep double-checking his work because I caught him trying to smuggle a rescue note out in one of the envelopes once. I have to weigh the envelopes each time and it was three grams heavier than it should have been, and when I opened it to check why, I found the note. I couldn't trust him after that. But I couldn't afford to stop doing it as it paid more per hour than my cleaning, so I took on the role. Now, I'm stuck doing this monotonous job day in and day out.

Eleanor knocks on the door ten minutes later.

'Come in.'

She opens and then peers round the door. 'Still want some help?'

'I've got one hundred envelopes with your name on them,' I say with a smile.

Eleanor ducks out quickly and then walks in holding two mugs. 'I made you a cup of tea.'

'That's very nice of you. Thank you.'

She sets the mugs on the floor and then sits cross-legged facing me. 'So ... what do I need to do?'

I explain how to check the details on the sheet, add the relevant papers to the envelope, then print out the label from the label machine and weigh them, making a note in the logbook. It's that simple.

She tells me about her day, and I listen without saying a lot until she mentions that the young man from the butcher's has asked her out for a drink tomorrow night. She asks me what I think that means. Having had no experience with the opposite sex other than the beatings I took from my father, and the difficult relationship I have with my brother, I don't have a lot of information to give her. But I want to help. It's almost like she's asking my advice about men as if I were her mother or older sister. I've never felt so valued before.

'This boy, Eric,' I say. 'Do you like him?'

'I mean ... he's fit, but ... yeah, I think I do.'

I hand her another stack of envelopes, which she takes and places by her side on the floor.

'He keeps asking how I'm settling in here with you.'

I don't respond directly, but I do say, 'He and his friends used to hang around here a lot when they were younger. I may have threatened them once or twice. Nothing bad, but maybe he holds a grudge against me.'

Eleanor smiles slightly. 'Can I ask you a personal question?'

I try not to react too much. 'Of course.'

'What happened to your parents and your brother?'

I knew this was coming. I already have a back story in place.

'My family did leave me twenty years ago. My father wasn't a nice man. He beat me and my brother almost daily. He owed a lot of money – gambling debts, you know – and drank heavily. One day, he received a letter from Australia. Basically, his great-aunt who had owned a huge farm there had died and left it all to him. Despite having a decent-paying job, my father couldn't keep the family home running here, so he decided to relocate to Australia and start afresh at the farm. I didn't want to go. My brother tried to convince me, but I refused. In the end, they left me here. They said I could sell the house if I needed the money, but I couldn't let it go. A few bailiffs came asking where my father was, and I told them, but after a while, things died down. My brother writes to me once a year, and I write back to him. My father died five years ago from cancer and my mother, as far as I know, is still over there. I don't hear from her at all, but my brother says she's settled and happy. My brother intends to stay in Australia on the farm. He has a wife and child now, a new life. I'm happy for him, but I do miss him terribly.'

I'm surprised how easily the lie trips off my tongue. Eleanor is the first person who has asked me about my family. Everyone else in the village has gossiped behind my back, spread rumours and made up their own stories about what happened. I anticipated the question from the start, which is why I came up with the story.

Eleanor looks at me with sadness in her eyes. 'So ... this house is the only thing you have left of your family.'

'Yes.'

'How come you've never got married or anything, or had kids?'

I smile as I place a sealed envelope on top of the ever-growing pile. 'Well, since everyone around here thinks I'm weird, it's been rather difficult to form any sort of relationship with anyone.'

Eleanor opens her mouth to answer, but then a slight vibration in the floor disturbs us, followed by a dull thud.

Kevin.

Sometimes he makes a lot of noise. I'm not sure why because no one – except for me, of course – will hear him. Maybe it gives him something to do, but now there is someone else in the house. I wonder if he has guessed that, that there's someone who could hear him. I look at Eleanor, wondering if she can hear the thumping. I think he bangs things against the walls, but then I realise he shouldn't be making noise right now because I gave him plenty of mashed-up sedatives in his early dinner.

'Can you hear something?' asks Eleanor.

I scramble to my feet. 'It sounds like the boiler in the basement is on the way out again. I'd better go and check. That's enough packing for tonight. I'll go and get dinner started once I've checked the boiler.'

'Would you like some help?'

'No, that won't be necessary, thank you. But how about

you take the rest of those envelopes to your room and finish them up there?'

Eleanor nods. 'Yes, okay.'

I wait while Eleanor gathers the envelopes. I watch as she enters her attic room before I storm down the stairs and enter the basement.

16

Elle

The weird thumping noise doesn't last long. Vera says it's the boiler, which just adds another layer of creepiness to this old house. I manage to finish stuffing and packing all the envelopes before dinner, which we eat in front of the television while watching another game show. We don't talk any further about her family, nor mine, but I feel positive about the fact she's shared details of her life. She's opening up to me and I'm grateful. She seems a little on edge and the further the evening wears on, the more I think there might be something wrong because her eyes continuously flick side to side, like a nervous mouse about to run from a hungry cat. Speaking of which, our evening is interrupted by a meow and scratching at the window. Vera lets Ollie into the house and he promptly curls up on one of the pillows on the sofa, every so often opening one green eye and glaring at me. I'm not sure I'm welcome in his home, but luckily it's not up to him.

I say goodnight to Vera and Ollie at around ten and head to bed. I think about Vera and her family as I climb under the covers, pulling them right up under my chin. I'm glad she still has contact with her brother, even though she hasn't seen him for so long. It saves me the job of finding him for her. If only the people in town wouldn't treat her like a criminal or some insane woman, more of a laughingstock than a human being.

The heating in the room is on low. I think Vera's been reducing it to cut down on costs, but I don't mind wearing an extra pair of socks to bed. She gave me a spare blanket to use too, which looks as if it's been handmade with scraps of old clothing.

As I drift off to sleep, my mind is filled with visions of monsters under my bed and dark shadows hiding in corners.

THE NEXT MORNING, I say goodbye to Vera who's doing another load of laundry and open the front door to leave for work. I go to take a step and freeze in place. Ollie is sitting on the doorstep, his tail swishing, but it's not him that's made me stop. It's the gross thing in front of his paws.

'Eww,' I say. It looks as if he's brought a dead mouse or something and placed it on the doorstep. I know cats do that sometimes. He meows at me. 'Delightful,' I say as I bend down to take a closer look. My stomach turns. It's not a mouse as I first thought, but it is a mass of bone and hair. There's no fur or tail.

'What the hell is that?' I ask him, covering my mouth, and holding back a gag.

He meows at me again.

I sigh. 'Vera won't be happy if you leave that thing on the doorstep.'

Ollie gives me one last meow, turns and struts away towards the back of the garage, clearly pleased with himself. I roll my eyes. 'Fine. I'll clear it up,' I mutter.

I run inside and grab a plastic bag, put my hand inside and reach down to pick up the offending item. The mass is a thin bone.

'Oh, my goodness, what on earth is that?'

'Ollie brought you a gift,' I say as I tie the bag handle in a knot. Vera appears behind me and takes the bag from me without asking.

'I'll dispose of that. He's disgusting. He's always leaving dead mice and birds lying around.'

'I don't think that's what that is,' I say, pointing at the bag. 'I couldn't work out what it was.'

'Never mind. Thanks for clearing it up. Have a good day at work.'

Other than my stomach feeling a little queasy, the walk into town is delightful. The ground is covered in a sprinkling of frost and with the sun shining, it causes the ice to sparkle all around me. My head's a bit cold, so I make a mental note to buy a warm hat soon. I wave at Laura as I pass her on the way to the café, and she glares back, but I don't stop because I'm already running late, thanks to clearing up the gift from Ollie.

The day passes by without any major incident, apart from accidentally spilling a cup of coffee down myself. Luckily, it covered the apron and not my jeans or jumper, which I'm wearing tonight to meet Eric. The chat I had with Vera last night and how it feels surreal, because it's the kind

of chat I've always wanted to have with my mum, but she
never spent the time to talk to me about boys, or even ask
me if I'm interested in them. There was a time when I was
at school where I thought I might be gay because I had a
huge crush on a girl in a different class, but I couldn't talk
to anyone about it. My mum never even told me about
periods until one day when I was thirteen, I started
bleeding and ran to her crying. She snapped at me and told
me to stop being silly, then simply gave me some money to
go to the shop to buy pads and tampons. I had to ask the
lady at the chemist's for help because there were so many
different brands, and I had no idea what to buy or how to
use them.

Eric arrives a couple of minutes before my shift is due to
end. He waves at me, and I wave back. He's made an effort.
He's wearing an ironed shirt with a warm jacket over the top
and a pair of snug jeans. I'm suddenly wishing I'd spent
longer than ten seconds this morning thinking about what
to wear. I'd chosen a plain T-shirt and jeans with a knitted
jumper. Vera and I still haven't been clothes shopping yet, so
this was the best I could come up with at short notice.

Eric walks me to the local pub, which is just down the
road. He holds the door open for me and we head to a table
in the far corner. This is the first time I've been inside a pub
or bar or anywhere they mainly serve alcohol. I'm aware I'm
underage, but it takes me a few seconds to remember that
Eric doesn't know that, and I have my fake ID that says I'm
eighteen.

'What can I get you to drink?' asks Eric.

'Oh ... um ... a Diet Coke would be great, thanks.'

Eric raises his eyebrows. 'You don't want a proper drink
to unwind after a long day at work?'

'Not right now, thanks.' I neglect to mention I've never drunk alcohol before, and I don't intend to start now.

'Okay,' he says, walking to the bar and placing our order.

I cast a glance around, taking note of a couple of other people who are enjoying a late afternoon/early evening drink and meal. I haven't been on a date for a long time. I'm not even sure if this is a date. Do I flirt with him? He seems so much older than me. If he knew I was under eighteen, would he even be interested? My mind is buzzing with questions, so I glance at my surroundings to calm my thoughts. The pub itself is homely, cosy with a log fire burning in the corner. There are low beams above with dozens of glasses and mugs, all of varying sizes and shapes, dangling from hooks.

'Here we go,' says Eric, placing a half-pint of Coke on the table.

'Thank you.'

He sits down opposite me, a glass of beer in his hand. 'So ... good day at work?' he asks.

'Yeah, not bad. Long, though.' I take a sip of Coke to quench my dry mouth. It tastes a bit weird. Maybe it's not the own-branded stuff I'm used to. 'I'm finally getting the hang of the coffee machine.'

He chuckles. 'Always a tricky thing to work out.'

I take another sip and put the glass down. 'Also, Vera and I are getting on great. She even let me dye her hair and give her a haircut.'

'Wow, that's amazing.' We spend a few seconds in silence and then he takes a deep breath. 'Where did you say you were from again?'

'Um ... Bath.'

'That's so weird.'

'Huh?'

'Well, I was watching the news the other day. There's this girl who's missing from Gloucester. Elle Walter or Walters, something like that. She's got long black hair and as soon as I saw her on the television, I thought she bore a resemblance to you.'

I almost choke on my Coke. 'Oh, t-that is weird.'

'Yeah, that's what I thought. And the other day, when I was in the back of the café with Carl, I happened to catch a glimpse of your ID. Sorry, I know that was wrong, but ... it's a good fake, I'll give you that.'

My mouth drops open. 'W-What? My ID isn't fake.'

Eric laughs. 'Elle, I know a fake ID when I see one. I had one when I was underage.'

Fuck!

It's all over. He knows who I am. It's hard to work out when he found out exactly or whether he's been piecing together the evidence from the start. He stares at me as he drinks his beer, holding eye contact.

'Don't look so scared, Elle. I've no intention of handing you over to the police. It's clear you haven't been kidnapped or are in any sort of danger.'

'Why bring it up then?' I'm on the defensive now. My guard is up. Should I run? There's no point trying to deny it.

He shrugs. 'Just wanted you to know that I know and that I'm fine with it. So, you ran away from home and have a fake ID. Plenty of kids do.'

'I'm not a kid,' I say. I down half my drink, feeling light-headed as I do so.

'Right. Sorry, I didn't mean any offence.'

'You're not going to tell Carl, are you? I really need this job. I've only got a few months till I'm eighteen.'

He holds his hand up. 'Have no fear. Your secret's safe with me.'

Somehow, I'm not sure I believe him.

FIVE MINUTES LATER, I've finished my drink and I'm feeling a bit dizzy. I haven't eaten since breakfast, and I worked through my break earlier to earn some overtime. Eric buys me another Coke. This time, I ask for full fat. Maybe a kick of sugar will help, but ten minutes later when I finish the drink, I feel worse.

I excuse myself and go to the toilet where I sip some water from the tap and splash my face. My legs wobble and I have to reach out to steady myself. Why do I feel so off-kilter? Why is the room spinning? I need to eat something, but my stomach is rolling and heaving. I don't think I've ever felt like this before, even when I had the flu.

When I stumble back to the table, there's another drink waiting for me. 'I'm sorry, Eric, but I'm not feeling too well. I'm going to head out. Thanks for the drinks.'

He stands up. 'Let me drop you off.'

'No, thanks. I'd rather walk.' And, in all honesty, I don't want to be around him any longer.

'Don't be silly,' he says. 'Here. Sit down. Have another drink.' He pushes the glass across the table towards me, and that's when the penny drops.

He's been spiking my drinks.

I'm drunk and it's taken me this long to figure it out because I've never been drunk before, so I have no idea what it feels like. I don't know what type of alcohol he's used but it must be strong, or maybe I feel like this because my body isn't used to the effects. Dizziness and nausea are prominent, and my mind feels numb, fuzzy, like I'm not in control of my own actions. People do this to themselves on purpose?

'You've put something in my drink,' I say slowly.

Eric sighs. 'Just vodka. I thought it might help relax you.'

'You've drugged me!' I shout, reaching for the back of a chair to steady myself, but I miss and stumble against the side of the table. The people on the table in the corner look up, but don't say anything.

'Shh! Keep your voice down. It's not like that. I wasn't going to take advantage of you or anything. I'm not like that. I just wanted you to relax and have a bit of fun, that's all.'

'I'm underage! It's illegal.'

'So? You've run away from home at seventeen. I'm betting that's illegal too, not to mention your fake ID. I thought a little vodka in your drink wouldn't matter that much to you in the grand scheme of things.'

I roll my eyes, but the action makes my dizziness worse. 'I have to go. Don't talk to me ever again. Vera was right about you.' I grab my jacket and head for the door. I manage to get outside before he joins me.

'Let me drive you home.'

'Go away!' I almost scream.

'Fine. Walk. I don't care.'

Eric turns and storms away, muttering something about me being a bitch. It's dark now and it's started to rain. My whole body shivers as I reach for my phone. There's no way I can walk home. Vera gave me her mobile number for emergencies, but I've never actually seen her with it, so I don't even know if she'll even answer.

I stumble a few steps, keeping the phone pressed to my ear as it dials. It rings out.

'Eleanor? Are you okay?'

'I ... I need help. He ... I ... feel funny.'

'Where are you?'

I look around me. 'The butcher's.'

'Stay there. I'll be five minutes.'

I hang up, but my fingers are so cold that the phone tumbles from my hand and lands in a puddle. The screen doesn't break, but the water will have done some internal damage. I bend down to pick it up, my head spinning. This is such a horrible experience. When does this feeling pass? I lean against the side of the building and then crouch down, my knees up against my chest. The rain is torrential, and it doesn't take long before I'm soaked to the skin.

'Eleanor!' I hear my name and look up as Vera stops the car and gets out. She kneels next to me. 'What the hell did that creep do to you? How much alcohol have you drunk?'

I want to answer, but I can't form the words. I start crying.

Vera puts her arm around me. 'It's okay. I've got you now. Let's get you home.' She helps me stand, walks me to the passenger side and gets me into the seat.

The short car journey is spent in silence. I'm so cold and dizzy that I barely register what's happening. It feels as if I'm in a dream as Vera leads me into the house. I wait by the basement door while she heads into the basement to switch on the hot water, then she leads me up the stairs and into the bathroom where she starts running a bath.

I shiver violently and lunge towards the toilet just in time as vomit explodes from my mouth. Vera strokes my back and speaks calmly to me as my stomach empties itself. She hands me a glass of water and a damp cloth when I'm finished. I wipe my mouth and take a sip. My head is still spinning, but I feel slightly better now I've been sick.

'I need to get you out of these wet clothes.'

I attempt to undress, but my fingers are still numb, and my body feels disconnected from my brain. Vera undresses me little by little and then helps me step into the warm bath. She then begins washing my hair, taking her time and being gentle.

'When you feel ready to talk, I need you to tell me what happened,' she says.

I keep my head down, staring at the bubbly bath water. I'm so ashamed, I can't even look at her. Once I'm washed, she helps me out of the bath, dries me and fetches a clean nightgown that I assume belongs to her. Then leads me upstairs to my room and tucks me into bed like I'm a sick child. She places a bowl next to the bed and some towels, then gently strokes my forehead.

'You get some sleep now. You're going to feel pretty bad when you wake up, but nothing some painkillers and water won't fix. Do you have work in the morning?'

I shake my head as my eyes close. I'm so tired. I just want to sleep.

THERE'S a low hum coming from somewhere. It stops and starts, never forming any sort of pattern. Several moments pass before my brain kicks into gear and I remember the events of last night. Or, at least, snippets of it. I remember the pub and feeling dizzy. I remember the rain and Vera putting me in the bath. That's about it. All the details in between are jumbled up.

Even so, the cold, hard fact of the matter is: Eric knows who I am and last night I pissed him off enough for him to storm away and call me a bitch. He said he wouldn't tell the police who I am, but does he mean it? Am I safe here? I can't risk it. I need to leave this village as soon as possible. The thought of moving on again fills me with such dread that tears swell in my eyes, and I let out a small sob. I don't want to leave. I'm happy and settled here; at least I was until last night. How could I have been so wrong about Eric? I was blinded by his good looks and his seemingly kind nature, but it was all fake, wasn't it? I don't believe for a second that he didn't mean to take advantage of me last night. My mind flickers on to Willow and her disappearance and what Stacey said about Eric being a suspect. Shit. Did he have something to do with Willow's disappearance? Given what he was prepared to do last night, I'm glad I managed to get out of there before things escalated, before I passed out. I had a lucky escape.

My head feels as if it's about to split in two. I force my eyes open, squinting against the faint light. There's a glass of water next to my bed and a packet of pills. I drink as if I've been without water for three days, then manage to choke down two paracetamol before collapsing back onto my pillow.

I don't want to get up and face reality. I'm so thankful I don't have an early shift, but I do have work later today. Despite a lingering swell of nausea in my stomach, I'm hungry, so I push back the bed covers and sit up, stopping to allow the dizziness to pass.

'I thought I heard you,' says Vera.

I look up and see her standing in the doorway. 'Vera ... I'm so sorry ... I don't know what happened.'

She sighs. I hate the thought of her being disappointed in me. She shakes her head. 'I knew that boy was bad news. Did you drink voluntarily?'

'No. He bought me a couple of Cokes at the bar. It tasted funny, but I didn't think anything of it. Then, I started feeling weird. He said ... I can't remember much, but I refused his offer to drive me home.'

Vera mutters something. Is she angry with me?

'I'm so sorry,' I say again.

'Why are you apologising? It's not your fault.'

'It isn't?'

'Of course not, you silly girl. That boy gave you alcohol without your permission. I should report him to the police.'

'No!' I shout, a bit too loud. 'Sorry ... No, please don't get the police involved.' This is all getting too real. I don't want to have to deal with any of it. I want to forget it happened.

'Are you sure?' Vera looks concerned, but there's also relief flickering behind her eyes. Maybe she doesn't want to get the police involved either. I nod and her shoulders relax. 'Okay, well, come and eat something if you feel up to it.'

I join Vera downstairs a few minutes later. She's made me a slice of toast with jam. She told me at first that I'd have to make my own breakfast as she was too busy in the mornings with her chores, but either she's completed them already, or she is leaving them to finish later. I slide my bum onto the nearest kitchen chair and begin to take small bites. I force down each mouthful, despite my stomach gurgling, but by the time I've finished the toast, I feel a bit better.

'Vera, I ... I don't think I can stay here anymore.'

'What do you mean?'

I hang my head, fighting back tears. 'Eric ... he ... knows something about me and I'm afraid he'll use it against me. I'm afraid I may be in danger if I stay here.'

Vera stares at me for a long time and says nothing. In the

end, I look up to make sure she's heard me and is still in the room.

'Does this have something to do with the black eye you had when I first met you?' she asks.

'Yes.'

'I understand.'

'Do you?'

'Yes, my parents ... Well, let's just say that you and I have that in common.'

'I'm sorry.'

Vera doesn't reply. She sits opposite me, reaches across the table and places a hand over mine. 'Eleanor, I promise I'll do whatever it takes to keep you safe, okay? You can trust me.'

I gulp loudly. 'Actually, my name's not Eleanor. It's Elle.'

Vera does a great job of hiding her surprise. 'In that case, Elle ... I don't want you anywhere near that boy again. I shall have a quiet word with his father. He owes me a favour,' she says, sounding suspiciously like my mum, even though my mum never showed that much concern for me.

I shake my head. 'I won't. I promise.'

'Promise me that you won't just leave without telling me, okay? I'm going to look after you now.'

'Thank you,' I say with a squeak as tears fill my eyes again.

'There's something you should probably know about Eric,' she adds. 'He was a suspect a few years ago in the disappearance of a young girl.'

My eyes widen. 'You mean Willow, Carl's daughter?'

'Yes, that's the one. They were dating at the time.'

'Yeah, I did actually hear that from Stacey. But I didn't think he was capable of something so awful. He seemed so nice. Even Carl likes him, so I assumed he didn't blame him anymore. Why didn't you warn me about him earlier when we spoke the other night?'

Vera sighs. 'You seemed to like him so much. Plus, he wasn't actually charged, so nothing ever came of it. And, as you say, Carl accepts he's innocent, so ... Anyway, I think you had a lucky escape, Elle. Like I said, I'll speak to his father first, but I won't mention anything else.'

I nod, too dumbfounded to say anything.

Vera seems satisfied to leave it there, even though she's clearly not happy about what Eric did. It's not like he attacked me or took advantage of me, but he could have done. It was wrong. He's a nasty piece of work and my stomach is already clenching with anxiety at the thought of running into him again. Maybe he'll have the sense to stay away from me.

Then again, maybe not.

What if Vera is too late? What if he's already told the police about me? What if he could really have done something to Willow?

17

26th January 2004

The next day, Vera threw the last load of blood-soaked carpet and clothes onto the bonfire that Kevin had lit at the end of their garden and watched it burn, her eyes glued to the crackle and pop of the orange flames as the ash rose into the air and was swept away in the breeze. There was no chance of saving the cream carpet upstairs, so they pulled the whole lot up, revealing the wooden boards beneath, and chucked it on the fire. Thick clouds of black smoke billowed into the sky, but luckily the wind was blowing it away from the village so it was unlikely anyone would notice.

Vera managed to scope out the cold room in the base-ment while Kevin was showering. She set up a bed and a bucket in the corner. She'd add more items when needed, but now she had to get Kevin inside somehow, but since

Kevin was adamant he wasn't hiding in there, she had to come up with another plan.

It didn't take long before Vera remembered her mother's sleeping pills in her bedside cabinet drawer. Often, her mother would take one, maybe two, to knock herself out so she couldn't hear her husband shouting at her children. Vera despised her for that, for ignoring their cries for help over and over, for never doing a thing to stop the abuse.

Vera crushed four tablets with the back of a spoon and dissolved the powder in a cold drink. Kevin kept talking about what they needed to do next. He had some hare-brained idea to run away, but with what? They had no money. They couldn't sell the house because it didn't belong to them, and they couldn't tell anyone their parents were dead because they couldn't show them the bodies. They'd have to leave the house and all its possessions behind and start with nothing. It didn't make any sense to her when they could stay here for a while and keep their heads down. Running away would only make them look guilty of a crime.

Vera let him talk and watched as he drank. A few minutes later, his speech slurred and his movements became slower. She waited until his eyes drooped closed and the empty glass tumbled from his hand onto the floor. Then she stood and got to work. He was heavier than he looked, but inch by inch she dragged him through the lounge, down the hallway, down the basement stairs and across the floor to the cold room. She failed in lifting him onto the bed, but laid him next to it, with a pillow under his head and a blanket over his body. The room was cold, but not freezing, but she would need to insulate it at some point or otherwise he'd freeze to death or at least catch pneumonia. Once Kevin had got used to his surroundings, he could help her with that.

Vera left him a glass of water and a ham sandwich. She removed the handle on the inside of the room so he couldn't open the door and installed a deadbolt on the outside. Kevin had showed her how to use a few tools over the years. He was good at building things and had practically taught himself; their father never spent any time with either of them to teach them any life skills.

Vera walked upstairs, closed the basement door, locked that too, and made herself a cup of tea, revelling in the silence that now filled the house.

An HOUR LATER, the banging and shouting started. Vera sat outside the cold room door on the floor with her back against the wall, her knees pulled up to her chest as she listened to her brother's shouts. She wasn't worried about him breaking down the door. It was solid, as were the walls.

'Vera! Let me out!'

'Listen to me, Kevin.' She didn't have to speak too loudly for him to hear her. The banging stopped. 'Just hide for a few weeks. That's all. I've got it all planned out. Your idea of running away was never going to work. You're a murderer, Kevin, whether you intended to be or not.'

'What do you mean? What have you planned out?'

'Look, I just want to protect you. All you have to do is stay in there for a few weeks while I sort things out. Then we'll be free to start a new life.'

A long silence followed her last word. So long, in fact, that she couldn't be certain he'd heard her, but then he said, 'Okay, fine. I'll stay in here.'

Vera breathed out and leaned her head against the wall.

Everything was going to be okay. She was protecting him. He was safe.

LATER THAT NIGHT, she knocked on the cold room door. She'd brought him dinner, which she'd cooked from scratch. Vera enjoyed cooking, despite never having been shown how to do it, but there were plenty of cookbooks in the kitchen she could follow. It was satisfying to cook a meal from scratch. She felt as if she'd accomplished something.

'I've brought dinner,' she said. 'Don't try anything silly.'

'I won't.'

Vera wasn't sure she could trust him, but she'd been clever. She'd removed the handle from the inside of the basement door to the hall as well and closed it. However, she had hidden the handle within the basement wall at the back, its location only known to her. Kevin wouldn't be able to escape. But she could, if for any reason she was trapped down here with him.

Vera opened the door, stepped inside the room, keeping the door open by standing against it. Kevin sat on the bed, his back against the wall with his legs stretched in front of him. He'd been in there by himself for just over eight hours.

'Hungry?' she asked.

'Starving.'

Vera took the tray with its two plates of food over to the bed and placed it next to him, then retreated to the safety of the door. She watched him eat, studying his every move. She had a knife tucked into the waistband of her trousers just in case he attempted to make a run for it.

'I love fish pie,' he said once every morsel was gone.

'Me too.'

'It's better than Mum used to make.'

'Thanks,' she answered with a smile. 'I'm sorry about all this. I promise you that in a few weeks, it will be safe to come out. You did a huge thing for me. You put yourself at risk. I want to return the favour.'

'Whatever. I can't believe you actually drugged me, though. What the hell?'

'Like I said, it's for your own good.'

'Whatever you need to tell yourself, Vera.'

ONE MONTH LATER, Vera had created a perfect routine for her and Kevin. But he was agitated and bored, so she gave him books, and she signed up to pack boxes and envelopes from home as a part-time job. It wouldn't be a long-term job, but Vera had a plan for that. She wanted to start her own cleaning business, yet whenever Kevin talked about getting out and away from here, her mind refused to think about anything else.

Vera was happy here. But letting Kevin out would mean extra risk, and it would upset the solid routine she'd built. She couldn't let that happen. Kevin would have to stay in the basement for a while longer. She didn't know how long. Maybe a year? The people in town hadn't talked a lot about her parents and Kevin disappearing. They didn't ask many questions. It was true; neither of her parents had been well-liked. Therefore, the village seemed okay with the fact they were gone.

Vera knocked on the door. 'Kevin. Breakfast.'

She waited for their agreed time of twenty seconds before opening the door. Kevin was on the bed in his usual position.

'Today's the day, right?' he asked.

'What do you mean?'

'I'm getting out today. You promised last week that you'd let me out today.'

'Did I?'

Kevin's eyes grew dark. 'Vera ... you promised. I've been in here for over a month.'

'You need to stay in longer. People are starting to talk. It's not safe. They're looking for you.'

'Why the hell would they be looking for me if you told them I moved to Australia with Mum and Dad?'

'They don't believe it. They are looking for their bodies.'

Kevin narrowed his eyes at her. 'I don't believe you.'

'It doesn't matter if you believe it or not. It's true. I need to keep you hidden. You'll be arrested for murder and locked up otherwise.'

'I'm already locked up!' Kevin exploded forwards off the bed. Vera stumbled backwards, dropping the tray of food.

'Kevin, I'm warning you. Stop. Please. Trust me, okay?' She held up her hands, palms facing him to show she meant no harm.

'Why should I trust you? You're dangerous.'

'I'm dangerous! You killed our parents. How do I know you won't kill anyone else? How do I know you won't kill me?'

Kevin laughed as he shook his head. 'You're unbelievable. Listen to yourself.' He stepped forwards, his fists clenched. 'Let me out. Now.'

Vera took a step backwards towards the open door, her only means of escape. 'No. Don't come any closer.'

Kevin lunged. Vera shrieked as he caught her around the

wrist and dug his fingernails into her skin. She yanked her arm away.

'Let go!' She swung her fist through the air and caught him in the jaw. It hurt her own hand more than she expected, but she hit him again. Then she grabbed the knife from her waistband and held it in front of her.

Kevin stumbled sideways, clearly not expecting her to fight back. He saw the knife and laughed. 'Fucking hell, Vera.'

Vera saw her moment to run and took it. She slammed the cold room door with a loud thud that reverberated around the basement, sending cascades of dust down on her head. Then she rested her forehead against the cool metal door and took a deep breath.

'Vera!' Kevin bellowed.

She didn't answer. Her wrist was on fire. Had he broken it? He'd managed to rip the skin with his nails when he'd grabbed her. Blood dripped down her arm.

He could stay in there and rot, for all she cared. He needed to understand why she was doing this. Why didn't he get it? She knew one thing for certain: she'd have to buy some handcuffs or a chain and tie him up if he was determined to keep trying to escape.

18

Vera

I drove Elle to work later that day and promised to pick her up at the end of her shift too, despite her saying she didn't need me to, but there was no way I was letting her walk home by herself. I can't trust anyone, especially that boy. What if he tries something else? I wouldn't put it past him. I've never liked him. I know she's afraid of him, but there's no way I'm letting her leave. Not now. Despite a few hiccups, I've enjoyed having her in my home. It's made the empty place feel homely again. She's awakened something in me that I never knew existed: a maternal instinct. Yes, I always wanted children, but I always assumed I'd make a terrible mother, considering the upbringing I had. But having Elle here is like finding a pool of clear water in an arid desert. That's why I need to keep her safe from that boy. His father won't help, so I'm taking matters into my own hands.

Elle's been very quiet all day. She went back to bed after eating breakfast, but said she felt better when I dropped her at the café. As I drive, I grip the steering wheel so hard my knuckles turn white. But, before driving home, I stop and make a quick detour at the butcher's shop.

There's no one behind the counter, so I step around and enter through the back door. The overpowering smell of raw meat is quite offensive to my nostrils, but I'm a cleaner, so I've dealt with much worse smells than this before.

I follow the grinding noise until I reach the room at the back where I find Eric. He's in a bloody apron and plastic gloves. He stops feeding meat into the machine when he sees me. The machine stays on, making a low whirring sound.

'Vera? What are you doing back here?'

'I need to speak to you about Elle.'

'Who?'

'Don't give me that. She told me that you know about her real identity.'

Eric puts down the meat and turns to face me. 'Okay, fine, I know about her.'

'I also know what you did to her last night.'

'I didn't do anything to her. She's lying. I didn't drug her. She got wasted by herself.'

I raise my eyebrows. 'Who said anything about drugging her, Eric?'

He responds with a laugh as he throws his head back. 'Okay, you got me. Look, I already told her that I won't tell anyone who she is.'

'I'm afraid I don't believe you. Just like I don't believe you had nothing to do with Willow's disappearance.'

Eric tenses and takes a step forwards. 'Excuse me?'

'You heard.'

'Vera, I don't know what you think you know, but you're wrong. You're nothing but a lonely old freak who needs to mind her own business.'

I hold my ground as he walks all the way up to me. He towers over me as I look up into his cold eyes. 'You've been a naughty boy, Eric,' I say with a smile.

Then, I reach my hand out to the side and grab the meat cleaver I saw on my way in, raise my hand and attempt to strike him, but he's too fast. He grasps my wrist tight and squeezes.

'I knew there was something wrong with you,' he sneers.

I don't have much time to react, but I kick out my foot and hit him in the shin. It's enough of a distraction for me to slice him across the stomach with the cleaver. He groans and doubles over. I move fast, lunge forwards and shove him hard.

He stumbles backwards, his arms flailing for something to grab. His left arm gets caught in the grinder and the horrible crunching sound makes me almost gag. He screams in pure agony as his arm is chewed up, inch by inch. He's making too much noise, but luckily the awful sound of the grinder is covering most of it, so I finish him off with the cleaver, clean across the throat.

Once he's stopped twitching, I turn off the machine, then make my way through the back of the shop.

. . .

I ARRIVE HOME SOMETIME LATER and head straight for a shower and then into the kitchen to begin preparing dinner. Since Elle is at work, I can take Kevin his food at the usual time of six this evening. He's been extremely stroppy every time I've gone in there. Maybe having his dinner on time will mellow him out a bit.

It's fish pie again tonight. His favourite, even though we don't usually have it on this day of the week. All the days are melting into one lately because my routine has changed and now I seem to be working around Elle's schedule. Therefore, mine is thrown out of whack.

I knock on the door and wait twenty seconds before opening. He sits on the bed, his back against the wall. I set his plate on the trolley and push it over to him, watching as he shuffles to the edge of the bed.

'On time today then,' he mutters as he begins to eat.

'Yes,' I say, folding my arms. I don't eat with him anymore. Plus, I've taken away his television privileges for a while.

'Why's that?'

'No reason.'

He stares at the food. 'Fish pie again?'

'You got a problem with that?'

He glares at me and shakes his head.

He eats without saying another word, which means that when a loud noise comes from upstairs, it's easily heard because I left the door open to the storage room. The basement door is shut, but that door isn't soundproofed so any sound made in the house can be easily heard from the basement.

'What's that?' he asks, looking up, his mouth full of pie.

Shit. What was that?

'Vera?' Elle's voice echoes through the house.

What the hell is she doing back so soon? I only dropped her off at work an hour ago.

Kevin's head snaps round to look at me. 'Who the fuck is that?'

I immediately turn and run out of the room, slamming the door. Elle's voice comes again as I pound up the stairs to the hall, my breathing laboured by the time I've reached the top.

'Elle?'

She appears in the kitchen doorway.

'What are you doing back from work so early?'

'We all got sent home. Carl closed the café early because something awful has happened and he's gone to help.'

'What's happened?' Elle looks terrible; she's been crying. She must have run here from the village. Her trousers are covered in mud splatters and her hair is wild, like she's been dragged through a hedge. 'Elle? Talk to me.'

'It's Eric. He ... He's been involved in an accident at work.'

My eyebrows raise slightly. 'What happened?'

'He was found by his dad. The saw they use to cut the meat must have malfunctioned. His arm got trapped and then he ... He's dead!' she wails, but there are no tears.

'That's awful,' I say.

Elle tilts her head sideways. 'Did you ... I mean ... After what we spoke about last night ...'

'You think I killed him?'

'No, I mean ... No, of course not.'

'It's a tragic accident, Elle. I'm very sorry he's dead, but this does mean you're safe now, doesn't it? Your secret is safe, so you can stay.'

'I guess so.'

A series of thuds sound from down below, so I pull the basement door closed. 'What do you plan to do for this evening, Elle? Dinner is ready if you'd like to eat now?'

'Sure. Thanks.'

I breathe out a sigh of relief. I'm not too sure if Elle believes me or not, but I can see she is relieved about her secret now being safe.

Elle walks with me to the kitchen while I dish up another plate for her. She sits and rests her chin in her hands, leaning her elbows on the table. I place a plate of fish pie in front of her and she responds by letting out a long sigh.

'Something wrong?' I ask.

'No. Thank you.' She takes a small bite. I sit opposite her, studying her mannerisms. I can't work out if she's upset or not over Eric's tragic accident. I feel like I should ask her about it, but just as I'm about to question her, the doorbell rings.

We both look at each other, waiting to see if the other says they're expecting company, but it was one of my rules right from the start. No visitors. Elle's expression tells me she's just as shocked as I am at the sound.

'Wait here,' I say, rising to my feet.

I can feel Elle's eyes on me as I leave the room. My heart pounds in my chest as I approach the front door. It's dark outside so I can't see an outline of a person on the doorstep. My brain frantically searches for an explanation as to who it could be. Whoever it is would have had to leave their car at the locked gate. They would have seen the signs, so they've obviously chosen to ignore them in order to come here to the door.

I grasp the handle and pull the door open a crack, peering out into the darkness.

A man stands on my step. He's dressed in a dark grey jacket, jeans and worker boots. His beard is greying, matching his hair. I don't recognise him, but I immediately don't like him.

'Who are you?' I ask.

'Are you Vera?'

My mouth turns dry. He knows me. 'Y-Yes. I'll ask you again. Who are you and why are you on my property?'

'I'm here for my daughter, Elle Walter.'

19

Elle

I push my plate away, my appetite disappearing, but to be honest, I haven't felt like eating since I heard about Eric. I know what he did to me was wrong and unforgiveable, but I wouldn't wish him harm because of it and I certainly wouldn't wish him dead in such a violent, terrifying way. I'm not sure why, but I keep thinking maybe it's my fault that he died. Maybe he was distracted at work and wasn't concentrating on what he was doing while using the machine that trapped his arm. Apparently, there was a lot of blood. Thinking about it makes my stomach turn over. Or maybe ... maybe it was Vera ...

Now, my focus is on who could be at the door. My first thought is the police, although I'm not sure why that's what I think of first. What would they be doing here? Unless they have come to ask us about Eric. Oh God, what if Eric told the police about me before he died and they're here now to take me back to my parents? I barely register as Vera stands up and walks into the hallway. I just continue to stare ahead and think of all the worst-case scenarios.

While Vera is answering the door, I stand up, walk to the sink and pour myself a glass of water. I listen to Vera ask in a stern voice, 'Who are you?'

Okay, so it's someone she doesn't recognise. That's bad.

I hear the deep voice respond and my stomach plummets like I'm riding a wild rollercoaster.

I recognise that voice. I'd recognise it anywhere.

No, no, no!

Vera asks again who the person is. I don't need to hear the response to know the truth. My dad has found me. Fear claws its way up my throat, ripping and strangling me as I let out a small whimper. I can't let him find me and take me away. No. This can't be happening.

My brain is telling me to run, but where? There's nowhere I can hide where he won't find me. How *did* he find me? Eric must have contacted him and told him where I was, bypassing the police entirely. He was the only person who knew my true identity, but then he had his accident. Was it an actual accident? Surely it has nothing to do with my dad being here.

It doesn't make any sense, but I don't have time to think about it. I need to hide. It's what I always do when it comes to my dad and the one place I hid where he never found me was the basement.

My eyes flick to the basement door. It's shut, but as I look at it I see that Vera must have forgotten to slide the deadbolt across and lock it earlier.

My eyes widen as I realise what this means. I'm saved.

The basement is my refuge. I can be safe there. I don't know what Vera will say to him or how she'll handle this situation, but if I hide, maybe she'll realise I don't want to go back home with my dad.

Vera is still talking to him, but their conversation is a blur because all I can focus on is the ringing in my ears and the thumping of my heart. It's so loud. I peer around the door-frame. Vera's body is blocking my view of his face. Maybe I can sprint across the hallway without him seeing me. I take a deep breath and hold it as I dash to the basement door. I forget about turning on the light, trip on the wonky step Vera told me about, and tumble to the bottom of the stairs. Luckily, the adrenaline is pumping around my body so much that I barely feel the bumps or the pain as I land awkwardly on my left ankle. The sudden stop winds me and I cough, gasping for breath.

There's enough residual light from the upstairs hallway to allow me to see across the basement. I need a place to hide. The shelving unit in the far corner is my destination.

I drag myself to my feet, gulping air. As I go to put weight through my left leg, a sharp pain erupts in my ankle. I gasp, but keep going, collapsing against the shelves. They're heavier than the unit in my old house, but with a bit of brute force, I manage to shift them away from the wall and squeeze behind, all the while ignoring the throbbing in my ankle, which is most likely badly sprained.

But ... Wait ...

There's a metal door back here.

What?

And a speaker with a button next to it.

I stare at the solid metal door hidden behind the shelves. It's obviously hidden. Now that I look at the shelves properly, the back of them has been boarded up so that no one can see the wall behind.

There's a handle, but also a huge deadbolt and padlock.

What the hell?

What's Vera hiding behind this door? Is this the reason she didn't want me coming down to the basement? Is she smuggling drugs or something? I shake my head, telling myself how ridiculous that sounds, but ... what is behind the door?

I crouch behind the shelves, my back against the door, listening for sounds or movement from upstairs. There is none. My breathing is too erratic and I'm gasping for a decent breath. I feel as if I've just sprinted a hundred metres.

That's when a scuffling noise begins. But it's not from upstairs.

It's from behind me.

Behind the door.

I hold my breath as I slowly turn and press my ear against the cool metal. All I hear is the pounding of my own heartbeat, but then ... another scuffle.

I raise my fist and knock three times, saying a silent prayer that no one answers, or I might just drop dead from fear. No one does answer, but the scuffle comes again, fainter this time.

Maybe it's a mouse.

Then ...

Light footsteps and the squeaking of metal, like bedsprings or a creaky door.

My blood runs cold as I cover my mouth with both hands, stifling a scream.

Vera has someone locked in her basement.

And now there are footsteps coming down the stairs.

20

Vera

The man on my doorstep stares at me in a way that makes the hairs on the back of my neck bristle. There's something about him that's setting off my internal alarm. This is Elle's father, but he's not here out of concern for her whereabouts or safety. He's not a doting father who's been worried sick about his daughter. There's an edge to his voice that is angry, annoyed. I think back to the bruise on her face the first time I saw her. He hit her. I know he did, and then she ran away from home. It all makes so much sense now.

But the fact he's here is something I wasn't expecting. It means that boy Eric told him where Elle was before his accident. Everything I've done, everything I've set up is about to fall apart. This can't happen. I won't allow it.

'You're Elle's father?' I finally manage to stutter.

'Yes. Where is she?'

'She's not here.'

'Bullshit. She's still a child. She ran away from home almost two weeks ago.'

I fold my arms across my chest. 'Why do you think she's here?'

'I had a tip off from someone around here.'

I squeeze my lips together, making a wild guess as to who that could have been. 'Well, she's not here anymore. She left.'

The man takes a single step towards me. 'You don't mind if I take a look around, do you?' He leans to one side to look behind me and frowns.

I lean in the same direction and block his view again. 'Actually, I do. Did you even see the signs at the gate? You're trespassing. Now, please leave my property or I'll be forced to call the police.' My heart rate increases so much that I struggle to take a breath.

'This won't take long.' The man pushes past me into the hallway, shoving me against the wall.

I'm so stunned by this move that I just stand there and watch as he surveys the area. 'Elle?' he calls out.

He stomps into the kitchen, calling her name over and over. My eyes dart to the side to where the cricket bat is mounted on the wall. My mouth is dry, so I lick my lips and swallow. I manoeuvre myself so I'm standing at the doorway between the hallway and the kitchen.

He's going to tear this place apart looking for her. He's going to ruin everything. The thought makes me hyperventilate. I put a hand against my heart and feel it racing. He glances down at the two plates of dinner on the table.

'You got company, have you?'

'Yes, now please leave.'

'I know she's here. You have two choices. Either I search this whole house and find her myself, or I call the police and report you for kidnapping my seventeen-year-old daughter. What's it to be?'

Neither of those choices are acceptable. I need to decide on what to do, and I need to do it now. He sneers at me. 'Fine, have it your way.' He goes to storm past me towards the hallway again.

Without thinking, I yank the cricket bat off its plinth and swing hard, smashing his skull. Blood explodes from the back of his head, and he collapses to the kitchen floor at my feet.

He's not dead, though. His foot's twitching and a gargling sound comes from his throat as blood pools around his head. I step backwards to avoid the puddle, then raise the bat above my head, bringing it down upon his skull once more.

Then again.

And again.

And once more for good measure.

I stand panting once I'm finished, the bat in my right hand, covered in matted hair, brains and blood. His body stops twitching and groaning, finally falling silent and still. Now I can breathe again.

As I stand over him, a calmness settles within me. Elle is safe. I only did it to protect her. I'd do anything to keep the people I love from harm. The same as what I'm doing for Kevin.

Kevin ...

Elle ...

Where is Elle? Maybe she ran and hid when she heard

her father at the door, but where would she hide? Then it hits me like a punch to the chest as I remember that I didn't slide the deadbolt across and lock the door earlier.

Still carrying the bloodied bat, I walk calmly into the hallway. The basement door is wide open.

My body shakes as I descend the basement stairs, being extra careful on the dodgy step. I flick on the light, scanning the room for a sign of a scared teenage girl. There aren't a lot of places to hide down here, but it doesn't take me long to notice that something isn't quite right.

Something looks different.

The shelving unit isn't sitting flush against the wall as it should be.

'Elle ... are you down here?'

There's no answer, as I expected. But she's here. I can feel it. I can practically hear her terrified heart beating.

I reach the bottom step and gently place the bat on the ground, barely making a sound. She's hiding from me now, which means she's found the hidden door. Whether she realises there's a person behind it is still unclear.

'Elle,' I say. 'Come out and we can talk. Your father is gone. You're safe now.' I wait for an answer, but none comes, so I try again. 'Elle, I won't hurt you. You can trust me.'

'Where's my dad?' comes the reply.

My eyes focus on the shelving unit. She's behind it. 'He's gone. I got rid of him. He won't hurt you anymore.'

A small, terrified face peers out from behind the unit. Her eyes are streaked with mascara. 'Why is there a door back here?' she asks.

'It's an old cold storage room,' I say with a kind smile. 'I don't think it's been opened in decades. My father used to keep meat in there. Sometimes whole animals he'd buy from the butcher's.'

Elle shudders as she stands; her legs are shaking and she has to use the shelving unit to hold herself steady, so she doesn't collapse. My immediate response is to throw myself at her and wrap my arms around her frail body, protecting her from everything. It's all I've ever wanted to do. Protect the people I care about and love. Like Kevin. And now, Elle. Because I do love Elle, even if it's in a different way than I love Kevin. She might not be my own flesh and blood, but she's in danger. I must save her.

I reach out my hand for her to take, but I realise too late that it's covered in splatters of blood. Perhaps my face is too. I didn't bother to check in the hallway mirror before I came down here. I don't want to scare her even more, but if she does notice the blood, then she doesn't mention it. She's a brave girl. She knows what's at stake.

'Come on,' I say. 'Let's go upstairs. It's cold down here. This basement always freaks me out.'

A low thud echoes from behind the door.

Elle and I lock eyes. Her pupils dilate.

It happens fast.

She makes a dash for the basement stairs, but her feet are moving too fast to get a proper grip on the concrete floor. Plus, she's limping as if she's injured. She slips, but quickly rectifies her stance, continuing her relentless effort to reach the top of the stairs. I lunge sideways, my hands outstretched, but miss grabbing her jacket by a mere two inches. She rushes past me, screaming, clawing her way towards the stairs.

Her feet reach the bottom step. I run after her, and she forgets about the wonky step. Everyone always does. I seize my chance, leap forwards, grab her hair and yank her backwards. I don't realise my own strength. She falls against me, her eyes wide with fear as she tumbles to the floor, the back of her head bouncing off the solid concrete.

She lies still at my feet as I assess the damage. Her head wound isn't bad. She's just unconscious. She'll be okay. Maybe a little sore when she wakes up, but what am I supposed to do with her now? I need time to think about my next move, and I can't think straight if I have to deal with Elle as well as everything else.

She must have heard the sound behind the door. Did she use the intercom before I arrived? Did she talk to Kevin? If so, what did he say?

No, no, no!

My chest heaves up and down as I attempt to quell the panic rising in me. Deep, steady breaths. In and slowly out on the count of three.

I can't let Elle leave this house without talking to her. I need to know that she won't tell everyone about Kevin. She won't know the details. She needs to understand.

I need to talk to her when she wakes up. Once she's calmed down, she'll be more receptive, I'm sure of it.

I make my decision, turn and unlock the hidden door.

'You knocked but you didn't come in within twenty seconds,' Kevin says when I enter.

It takes me a few moments to understand what he means. Elle must have realised someone was alive behind the door and knocked. That's why she ran. But once I've explained my story to her properly, she'll understand I've only done it to protect my brother. I know she'll understand my reasoning. She's a smart girl. She just needs to calm down from the shock of finding out her father had tracked her down. It must have been terrifying to hear his voice at the door.

'What's going on?' asks Kevin. He's on the bed, as he should be.

I don't answer him, but quietly turn and fetch Elle. She's a lot easier to drag than Kevin had been. I'm as gentle as I can be as I pull her through the door into the room.

Kevin's eyes are like saucers. 'Oh my God ... Vera ... What have you done? Who the hell is that?' Kevin shuffles towards the edge of the bed, but I immediately stop and hold up my hand.

'Stay back!' I shout. I don't trust my brother. This is the first human being he's seen in twenty years other than me.

Kevin does as he's told and remains seated as I drag Elle into the furthest corner away from him and lay her down so she's comfortable. She'll be safe here. He can't reach her because his chains aren't long enough. I'll be back for her later. There are a few things I need to do first.

'You're not just going to leave her in here, are you?'

'Relax. It's just to make sure she doesn't escape.'

'Vera ... I'm worried about you.'

I stifle a laugh. 'It's not me you need to be worried about, dear brother.'

'You've kidnapped a child!'

'I haven't kidnapped her. She's been living here of her own free will for over a week now. And she's not a child. She's almost eighteen.'

'What?'

'You have no idea, do you, Kevin? You have no idea the lengths I've had to go to keep you safe, to keep this house, to keep up with the bills. We've almost lost this house several times. I've had to work two jobs since you decided to be stupid enough to try and smuggle notes into the envelopes you were stuffing.' I point at my chest. 'I have kept us safe!' I shout. 'Me! I had to bring in Elle to help pay the bills. I had no choice.'

Kevin sighs as he shakes his head. 'Look at you, Vera. Look what you've done. If you'd listened to me at the start, then none of this would've happened. You say everything you've done has been to protect me ... Well, I've got news for you, dear sister. I'm the one who's been protecting you all these years.'

My shoulders sag and I force myself to take a deep breath as I'm at risk of hyperventilating if I don't. 'What are you talking about? You've been locked in this room for twenty years. How could you possibly have been protecting me?'

Kevin appears to have forgotten about the unconscious girl on the floor as he focuses all his attention on me. I don't like the way his eyes are burning into my soul. My twin brother doesn't look the same as how I knew him twenty years ago. Then again, I barely recognise myself either.

'You still don't remember anything, do you?'

'Remember what?'

'That night. Twenty years ago.'

I narrow my eyes at him. 'You killed our parents by bashing their heads in. That's what happened.'

Kevin sighs. 'No, Vera ... That was you.'

PART III

21

25th January 2004

The door swung open and slammed against the wall, only missing Kevin's face by a couple of inches. He jumped back and hid out of sight in the corner behind the door as his father stormed into the room, eyes blazing and fists clenched.

'Where is it?' he demanded.

Vera pulled the sheets further up to her chin. 'What are you talking about?'

'The bracelet I gave your mother is missing. Where is it?'

Vera's mouth turned to dust. She quickly slid her left hand under the sheet. 'I haven't seen it.'

'Don't lie to me,' he said with a hiss. He stomped further into the room. 'It stinks in here, girl. Have you even had a shower since you've been lying in your own filth? And I pay good money to heat this fucking house. The least you could do is keep the windows shut!' He pulled the window closed with such force that the picture hanging on the wall above Vera's head fell.

She shrieked as it hit her, raising both arms above her head in defence. She knew it was the wrong move as her father leapt towards her and grabbed her wrist, squeezing it so tight she thought it might snap in half.

But she didn't make a sound.

'Thief! You stole it!'

'No! I didn't ... I didn't ...'

'Don't lie to me!' With his other hand, he slapped her across the face. The noise his open palm made against her cheek sounded like a gunshot in her head. The room spun as her vision distorted and she fought against the urge to slip into darkness.

Vera opened her eyes and saw Kevin cowering in the corner behind the door, shaking his head. She didn't blame him. If he got involved, then he'd be beaten too. They'd both learned to stay put and not make a sound when the other was beaten. It wasn't worth them both taking their father's brute force.

Her father hit her again. And again.

His fists pummelled into her weak body like he was tenderising a piece of meat. She wasn't sure how much more she could take. She'd been hit before, many times, but this was the worst yet.

She cried out, tears streaming from her eyes and snot running from her nose, begging him to stop, but he didn't. Kevin sobbed in the corner, covering his head with his arms, rocking backwards and forwards. He had turned into a frightened little boy at the sight of his sister being beaten so viciously.

Then her mind snapped like a twig. It had been on the verge of breaking for a long time and now it finally happened, having been pushed to breaking point for far too long.

It was like a roaring fire had been lit in the middle of a black abyss. The relief was instantaneous, glorious. She spat the blood from her mouth and yelled 'Stop it!' at the top of her lungs. Her shrill scream filled her bedroom and spilled out into the hallway, shaking the walls. Kevin covered his ears.

And her father stopped hitting her.

'What the fuck?' He stepped back from her. Was that fear highlighted in his dark eyes?

Within seconds, her mother stormed into the room, carrying her father's prize cricket bat above her head. Her breath was ragged and frantic, and her livid eyes were searching the room.

'What the hell was that awful noise?' When she saw Vera on the floor, her face ablaze with fury, she frowned. 'Vera ... was that you?'

'What the hell are you doing with my bat?' shouted her father.

'I thought someone had broken in,' replied her mother.

'No, it was me,' said Vera, her voice strong, stern.

Her mother looked down at her. 'Get up, you silly girl.'

Vera rose to her feet in slow motion. The pain was there, pulsing through her body, but it was not where her mind was focused. Her fever no longer burned, but she still had a white, hot rage burning inside her, a rage she needed to extinguish or she feared she might self-combust.

'Kevin, get out,' she said.

Kevin peered past his fingers at his sister. 'V-Vera?'

'Get out!'

Kevin didn't need telling twice. He hauled himself to his feet and ran out of the room, slamming the door behind him. Vera's father turned to her; his fists were clenched.

'You snivelling little bitch,' he said with a throaty growl. 'Give me that bat, Marianne. I'm about to teach our daughter a lesson she'll never forget. Maybe a couple of broken legs will make sure you never talk back to me again.'

Her mother slowly held out the bat, but Vera was quicker. She darted forwards and snatched it from her mother's grasp, spun round and held it above her head, grasping it tight with both hands as if she were about to make a swing.

A scream came from her lips, even louder than before as she hurtled forwards.

She swung the bat and whacked her father straight across the face, cracking his jaw in two.

Her mother didn't even attempt to fight back or defend him. She ran from the room, shrieking for Kevin to come, shrieking for Kevin to help, but Kevin never came.

Vera watched as her father groaned and rolled over on the floor, his jaw broken and bleeding, his teeth smashed and his blood splattering across the walls.

'What was that, Dad?' she asked, stepping up to him. She leaned over his body. 'Sorry ... I can't quite make out what you're saying.'

Her father glared up at her, so much hatred in his eyes, but there was nothing he could do except let out a muffled scream as she brought the bat down on his face again. Not once. Not twice. But over and over and over until her arms burned with the physical effort of it all.

Blood, brain matter and shards of skull flicked up and over Vera as she let loose, striking her father's face until it was nothing more than a bloody pile, which oozed and soaked into the cream carpet. When she finally let the bat drop to her side, completely spent, she took a breath, inhaling the sweet, pungent aroma of fresh blood.

Vera turned and looked over her shoulder at the open door.

She stepped across the soaked carpet, her bare feet squelching through the viscous liquid.

She reached the landing and looked down, listening for any movement. Vera began her search of the house, opening each door slowly and ensuring she had looked in every possible hiding place before moving to the next room. She moved with purpose, carefully and deliberately, not rushing, but enjoying the adrenaline pumping through her body, invigorating it.

Reaching out her hand, she slowly locked the front door and any means of escape, hiding the key in the plant pot beside the door.

She found her mother cowering in the pantry. 'Hello, Mummy,' she said, reaching forwards and dragging her out by her hair.

'Vera, I'm sorry. I should have protected you from your father,' her mother whimpered. 'Believe me, I've tried so many times.'

Vera didn't reply; she just stared at the woman cowering on the floor. She didn't blink, not even once.

'Vera? Vera ...' Her mother's voice grew dimmer and dimmer.

The next thing Vera knew was her mother was shoving her to the side. She stumbled against the wall as her mother sprinted past her, screaming, and bolted to the front door. She yanked on the handle, but the door held firm.

Vera watched her mother attempt to open the door, but panic had well and truly set in. She turned and ran up the stairs, her only other option.

Vera followed, dragging the bat behind her, leaving bloody streaks on the floor of the kitchen and hallway. She placed each foot precisely in the centre of every step as she climbed the stairs, the bat thumping against each step behind her. She found her mother sobbing in her room, crouched over the mutilated body of her husband.

'What have you done? What have you done!'

Vera entered her bedroom. 'I've saved us,' she said.

Her mother opened her mouth to scream, but Vera silenced her with one swift blow to the head. She bashed her mother's body until bones cracked through the skin in her arms and legs. She landed on top of her husband with an awful thud, her arms draped over him, as if giving him one last embrace.

When Vera finally stopped, she dropped the bat and stood in the middle of her room, over the bodies of her parents, and stared at the open door, her eyes unmoving and unblinking.

She remained there, without moving a muscle, for over an hour before Kevin found her, but he couldn't wake her from whatever trance she was in. She'd retreated inside her mind, to a place of safety.

22

Elle

My body jerks awake as if I've been electrocuted and my eyes spring open. The first thought that comes to mind is thank God that was only a dream, but then my senses start switching on one by one. Pain receptors. White-hot pain in the back of my head and the throbbing pulse of blood pumping through my body. I can actually hear it travelling through my veins; it's the weirdest sensation I've ever experienced. Dizziness overwhelms me as I blink my eyes, attempting to focus on the ceiling. My eyes struggle to stay open at first, as if a heavy weight is dragging my eyelids closed. It's dark, dirty and the air feels and smells stagnant, like there's been no fresh air in here for a very long time.

Where the hell am I?

Am I actually in hell?

Then it comes crashing back to me in one quick swoop. Vera. My father. The basement. The hidden door.

I tried to escape and then ...

That part wasn't a dream.

I turn my head slowly to the left, wincing at the small movement. Tears leak from my eyes, but I don't wipe them away, preferring to feel them trickle down my cheeks in small rivers. A dark, tall shape emerges in front of me.

A man.

He's sitting on the floor, cross-legged, about five feet away, next to a metal bedframe and filthy mattress. His beard is shaggy and knotted and his hair reaches to his chest, greasy and wild. Flecks of grey weave through his dark hair. His clothes are filthy and look two sizes too big. The skin on his face is so pale, he's like a real-life vampire, devoid of all minerals and vitamins, as if he's never seen a ray of sunshine in his life. His teeth are yellow and uneven. His overgrown hair and beard cover his face, making it difficult to guess his age.

He hasn't made a single movement towards me, but the shock of seeing him there, in the flesh, a skeleton with skin on, sends waves of panic through me, emanating in a high-pitched scream. The kind of scream that always annoys me in horror movies.

The sound seems to upset him because he shuffles backwards on the bed towards the wall, covering his ears with his grubby hands, which have long, pale fingers ending in yellow, ragged fingernails.

'Stop!' he shouts.

His voice is oddly strong, and it does make me stop screaming. I push myself to a seated position and then copy his previous movement of shuffling as far away from him as possible until my back is against the far wall.

'Where am I? Who are you?' I ask in a rushed whisper.

The man slowly lowers his hands from his ears. 'What did you say?'

I gulp and speak again, this time a little louder. 'I said … who are you?'

'My name's Kevin.'

I close my eyes and take a deep breath. Oh my God. I should have seen it straight away. His eyes are the same as Vera's, but that means … That means … What, exactly?

Why the hell is Kevin locked in here? Is he sick? Violent? Oh my God … am I in danger? Is he going to kill me?

'How long have I been in here?' I ask for no other reason than to distract myself from the rising panic in my chest. My hands go to my hair and I start twiddling it through my fingers, immediately feeling slightly calmer.

'You've been unconscious for about three hours. I was beginning to think you might not wake up.'

Three hours? So, where the hell is Vera?

My mouth is dry. I lick my lips and swallow, attempting to kick-start my saliva glands, but there's no moisture to be had. The thirst I feel is almost unbearable, like I haven't had any liquid for days.

I lick my lips again. 'Water.'

'There is none. We have to wait until Vera feeds us.'

'When is that?'

'Vera hasn't exactly been keeping to our usual schedule lately … and now I know why.'

I rest my head against the wall, but don't close my eyes. Instead, I stare at Kevin, studying him, wondering what the hell he must be thinking right now. Is he as freaked out as I am?

'Are you going to hurt me?' I ask.

'If I wanted to hurt you, I would have done so by now. Besides ...' He reaches down to his left ankle and yanks on the thick metal chain. I hadn't even noticed it before, although I can't deny I'm relieved that he's chained up, if only for my own safety, which then makes me feel sorry for him. The skin around the metal cuff is red raw under the hem of his dirty trousers. I follow the chain with my eyes and see that it's securely fixed to the wall. I gather, from the length of the chain, that he wouldn't be able to reach me, even if he tried.

'How's your head?' he asks. His gravelly, deep voice tells me he doesn't have a lot of practice speaking out loud.

I reach my hand behind my head and then check my fingers for blood, but there is none. There is, however, a bump on my scalp, which hurts when I press down on it.

'It hurts, but there's no blood.'

I close my eyes against the dizziness and nausea.

Every brain cell tells me I should be afraid of this man. Anyone in their right mind would be after waking up locked in a small room with him. I try to stay calm, knowing that my energy is needed if I'm going to have any chance of defending myself or of escaping.

I take a glance around the room, taking note of a locked cupboard, the bed and mattress and a wheely trolley. There's what looks like a CCTV camera mounted above me, pointing down onto the bed and a black bucket with a board over the top, from which emanates a smell that assaults my nostrils. I don't even want to think about what's in there. I need a wee badly, but there's no way in hell I'm going to use that bucket. I'd rather wet myself.

'So, Elle ... What brings you to my humble abode?'

'How do you know my name?'

'Vera told me when she dragged you in here.'

A shudder ripples through me at the thought of being unconscious in this room with him.

'I don't understand why I'm here. Why am I locked in here with you?' I ask, shaking my head. 'Vera was my friend. She was nice to me. But she's been keeping you locked in here ... Why? How long have you been down here?' Even before he gives me the answer, I know it. By the state of him, it's not like he's been down here for just a few days.

'Twenty years.'

'B-But why?'

'What has she told you about me?'

I force my muddled brain to think back to the other night when we stuffed the envelopes in her room. The story of her parents and brother. She told me they left her and moved to Australia, and that she still heard from her brother from time to time. Her father had died and her mother was in a care home.

'She said you moved to Australia twenty years ago with your parents.'

Kevin chuckles. 'My sister, the avid storyteller.'

I pull my knees to my chest, ensuring I'm as far away from Kevin as I can get in this small space. Despite Vera telling me it's a cold storage room, it's not particularly cold, just stale. The walls appear to be padded. Kevin must notice me looking around inquisitively because he answers my silent questions.

'Over the years, Vera's done a lot of work to this room to

keep me secure. First, she padded it out and ensured it was warm and after about a year she made it soundproof.'

My stomach drops. Soundproof? How did she even do it? Vera doesn't strike me as someone who's good at DIY. Did Kevin help her in some way? Perhaps she somehow convinced him to help her build his own prison.

'Is it completely soundproof?' I ask.

Kevin shakes his head slightly. 'No room is completely soundproof. Not a makeshift one anyway. She doesn't know, but I've had a little helper over the years.'

This piques my interest. A helper? In here?

Kevin puts his finger to his lips, signalling to be quiet. I listen, holding my breath and then it appears. Faint shuffling and ... a tiny squeak.

A mouse.

'A few years ago, it started using the padding in the walls as nest-building material and now there's a hole in the soundproofing behind my bed. I sometimes shout through it and knock the metal bedframe against the wall. I know it's utterly pointless because Dawn House is very isolated, but it gives me a glimmer of hope from time to time that someone, somewhere, might hear me.'

'I had a spider friend called Trevor.' Kevin tilts his head sideways, probably wondering if I've lost the plot. 'I used to hide in the basement at home a lot. I felt safe down there,' I add.

He doesn't ask any further questions, which I'm thankful for. The truth is, I have no idea how to talk to him, or if I even want to hear what he has to say. All I want to do is get out of this room, this house, and then run away again. Vera isn't the woman I thought she was. She's sick. She's deluded. How could she do this to her own brother? Despite my desperation to escape, I do need to know what happened. I can't leave not knowing the truth.

'Why are you down here, Kevin? Why has she kept you locked up like this?' I think I know why, but I'm curious as to whether he'll reveal the truth or feed me a pack of lies to try and protect himself.

Kevin reaches forwards and picks at his big toe on his left foot. Both his feet are filthy, as if he's walked through soot and his toenails are yellow and overgrown, curling over on themselves. Does Vera not even give him the option to keep himself clean? I try not to screw up my nose in disgust as I watch him pick at his feet, peeling off dead flakes of skin.

'It's a long story,' he says. Then he looks up to the camera at the top corner of the room above my head. 'She's watching us, you know. Always watching.'

I swallow the lump in my throat. I might be able to use that to my advantage soon, but I still need to know the reason why she has kept her brother trapped down here like a caged animal.

'Tell me what happened.'

'Why do you want to know? I don't know you. You're the first person I've seen in twenty years. This could all be some elaborate scheme my sister has cooked up to trick me.'

'Trick you into doing what?'

'I don't know, but I stopped trusting Vera a long time ago. Whatever comes out of her mouth is a lie.'

'So ... tell me the truth. Set the record straight.' I sound more confident than I feel.

Kevin narrows his eyes at me. Then, he scans me from head to toe, which sets off all my internal alarms. I feel his eyes stop on my boobs. He's a grown man who's never seen another woman other than his sister for two decades, and

I'm trapped in a tiny room with him. God knows what's going through his mind right now. There's nothing in here I can use to defend myself. I just hope that the chain around his ankle is strong enough to hold him if he decides to attack. He's been starved of any sort of physical interaction with the opposite sex for his whole adult life. I doubt he's picky.

'Our parents were not good parents,' he says, dragging his eyes from my body. I feel violated already. 'Our father beat us, and our mother let it happen. Vera used to get it the worst. On our sixteenth birthday, he attacked her in her bedroom. Something inside her snapped. I should have done something, but I was frozen in fear. She told me to run. I did. I hid down in this basement for over an hour before emerging. I was afraid of what I'd find. I thought maybe our father had finally gone too far and killed her because ... there was silence in the house and blood smears across the landing and up the stairs.' He stops and stares at the floor beneath his feet.

I wait patiently for him to continue, barely taking a breath.

'I followed the blood and found Vera standing over the bodies of our parents. Except ... they were more like mounds of flesh and blood. She was in some sort of trance. Catatonic. She was just standing there holding the bat by her side, staring at the door. She didn't even blink an eye when I spoke to her, shook her and tried to wake her up. She just kept standing there, so ... I made my decision. I loved my sister. I didn't blame her for killing our parents. They deserved it.'

Kevin inhales and looks at me. 'I dragged the bodies down the stairs and outside behind the garage. I left Vera where she was because she wouldn't snap out of whatever trance she was in. I took the bat from her hand and took it with me. Then, when I came back inside the house, she was at the bottom of the stairs looking confused. She didn't remember what happened. She remembered our father hitting her, but after that, nothing. She was unstable. We buried them behind the garage, cleaned up the house, but then she got this idea in her head that she needed to protect me and hide me until things blew over.' Kevin shook his head. 'She drugged me, and I woke up in here.'

A million questions jostle for top position, but the only one that I manage to say is, 'Have you ever tried to escape?'

He looks at me as if I've spoken to him in a different language. 'Of course I have, but Vera's clever. She has devised all these things over the years to keep me here. The locks on the insides of the doors are removed, so even if I did get out of these chains, I wouldn't be able to open the door from the inside, in here or the basement door. I bet she's been keeping an eye on you since you've been here too.'

My thoughts turn to the garage and that day I went behind it and saw Ollie digging. Oh my God ... that thing he dropped on the doorstep. Was that ... a piece of a dead body? Bile fills my mouth, but I swallow it down.

Then I remember how often Vera appeared out of nowhere and surprised me. She has been keeping tabs on me. She must have been very desperate to invite me to live with her, knowing how much of a risk it was to have someone else living in this house with Kevin locked downstairs. Because of her desperation, she's dangerous. I can't trust her at all now.

I need to get out of here, but how? Would she really keep me down here with him? She must realise that I'm in danger.

She's not prepared for me to stay down here too. She probably panicked when she found me in the basement and
threw me in here until she could come up with a plan.

She'll need to feed me at some point. My stomach
gurgles as I think of food. Sooner or later, she'll come to the
door and maybe I can convince her to let me out. I won't tell
anyone. I'll just leave and never come back.

I have to try something.

Kevin and I stare at each other for a long time, neither of
us quite sure if we should trust each other.

23

Vera

I make myself a strong mug of sugary coffee and sit down at the kitchen table, avoiding the puddle of blood that's seeping across the tiled floor, snaking its way in between the grout. Elle's father's body is twisted at an unnatural angle, his head smashed in, brain matter exposed. I cover my nose with my hand, as the nauseating aroma of blood tickles it. The man's face isn't recognisable anymore.

I take a sip of coffee and spend a few moments gathering my thoughts, ignoring the dull ache of hunger in my stomach. This was not how I imagined the day would end. I don't even know what the time is, but it's irrelevant. The point is that there's a dead body on my kitchen floor, staining my lovely tiles and an extra – alive – body now locked in my basement. And neither of them is supposed to be there.

A meow makes me turn my head to the left. Ollie struts

in and enters the kitchen. How did he get in? He freezes when he sees me, but then tiptoes closer to the body, sniffing and then licking the spilled blood.

Delightful.

'Life would be much simpler if it was just you and me, wouldn't it, Ollie?'

The cat squawks and resumes lapping.

I'd better check on Elle and see if she's ready to listen to me. I don't have a plan, but I need to talk to Elle and make sure she's okay. Then I'll deal with the body of her father. When I closed the door on her, she was still unconscious, and I'm not sure how long it's been since I left her there.

I knock three times and press my ear close against the cool metal. I press the buzzer on the wall next to the door and speak into it. It's a system I set up years ago so that I could hear inside the room as long as I kept the buzzer compressed. 'Elle, are you okay?' I hold the buzzer and wait.

'What do you think?' comes the reply.

'Is your head all right?'

'No, it hurts. Vera ...'

'Yes, Elle.'

'Please let me out.'

'I'm afraid I can't do that right now. However, if you're ready to listen, then I'm ready to explain a few things.'

'Let me out first and then I'll listen.'

I let go of the buzzer and sigh. This isn't going to be easy. She's a strong-willed girl. If I open the door then she might ambush me and try to escape. I could shut the basement door and hide the handle like normal, but then what? We'll both be trapped down here. Plus, I reckon she's small enough to fit through the tiny window near the ceiling if she put her mind to it.

I press the buzzer once more. 'I'm sorry, Elle. I really am. I never meant for you to get involved in any of this. It wasn't my intention. Kevin is dangerous. I have to keep him locked up for his safety and for other people's safety.'

Eerie laughter comes through the intercom. Kevin can hear me. 'Still telling yourself that old chestnut, are you, Vera?' he shouts.

I grit my teeth, determined not to engage in an argument with my brother. It isn't about him right now. It's about making Elle understand my actions.

'If he's so dangerous then open the door and let me out,' says Elle.

'He's chained up. He can't hurt you as long as you don't get too close.'

More laughter from Kevin. 'Yeah, don't get too close, Elle.'

'I need to use the bathroom.' There's an urgency in her voice that's making me nervous. She's coming up with every excuse she can, anything to get me to let her out.

'There's a bucket in there. Ask Kevin to let you use it.'

'Fat chance,' shouts Kevin.

'I'd rather die,' responds Elle.

I stamp my foot. 'I can't open this door until I know you won't run. Even if you got out into the basement, remember what I told you about the door? It can't be opened from this side.'

'I remember. I won't run, I promise. Can we just talk outside?'

I let go of the buzzer. I want to trust her, but I can't. It's too easy. She's pretending to be understanding so that I'll open the door. She needs to stay in there until she realises that I have the control, the power. There is no escaping that room. Kevin knows that. Now, she needs to know it too.

'I'm sorry, Elle. But you need to understand.' I don't press the buzzer so she can hear, but instead I'm speaking to the empty basement. I hang my head, turn and push the shelving unit back in place before leaving the basement and sliding the deadbolt across.

THE DEAD BODY on my kitchen floor is disturbing me. I can't cook in these conditions. I keep having to sidestep the oozing blood, and at one point I trip up on his outstretched purple hand. Enough is enough. The body needs to get out of my kitchen. It's not sanitary.

Unfortunately, I don't have my brother to help me this time. He was the one who'd dragged our parents down the stairs and out behind the garage, and I remember how difficult it had been to drag Kevin's unconscious body down into the basement twenty years ago. Elle's father is much bigger than Kevin was. He's a full-grown man, weighing at least double what I do.

I don't have a choice.

Leaving the sausages to cook in the oven, I don some yellow rubber cleaning gloves and my apron and step up to the side of the body. I grab both his arms and pull, surprised at how stiff he is already, and lean back as far as I can. He moves an inch. I can't help but think that the crime dramas I sometimes watch don't portray how heavy bodies are for normal people to move. They make it look so easy.

It takes me over half an hour of puffing and panting and several breaks to drag the body out of my kitchen and into the hallway, partly because every time I manage to move him a few feet, I stop to clean the blood streaks he keeps leaving on my tiled hallway floor. Then I realise that the bins need emptying, and I have to rinse and refill the mop bucket. I pour the bloody water down the sink and use the thick bleach plus a splash of floral disinfectant for that springtime scent.

The sausages are burning. I can smell them from the hallway, so I quickly turn off the oven and survey the mess I still have to clean. Blood, plus a few bits of brain and teeth still decorate the white tiles in the kitchen. Dinner will have to wait a while longer; there's no way I can stomach eating next to such carnage. And it still stinks in here too, like decay and shit.

It takes another forty minutes to clean the kitchen using all the bleach, cleaning products and odour-eliminating products I own. Eventually, once the kitchen and hallway are sparkling, even cleaner than they were before, I wrap black bags around the body, ready for when I have the energy to move him again. I'm thinking he'll probably join my parents behind the garage. It seems a good a place as any to let him rot.

Finally, I sit down and eat the dinner I've prepared of sausages and mashed potatoes. I have made enough for Kevin and Elle, but still have no idea how I'm going to deliver the food to them. Elle is a loose cannon. If she wants to eat and drink, then she's going to have to behave. We shall see how hungry and thirsty she is.

Before I head down to the basement to attempt to feed them, I walk upstairs to my bedroom to check the camera feed before I open the door to ensure Elle is away from the door. I can't just take her word for it that she won't ambush me. It's an old camera system, so it's hard wired from the monitor in the basement room, and I keep the feed hidden underneath my dressing table.

I pull it out and switch it on, tapping my fingers on my knee while I wait for the grainy picture to load.

My heart stops.

Elle is lying on the floor with an arm across her chest, her hair covering her face. She's at such an unnatural angle that she can't be asleep. She's at the foot of the bed and …

My heart lurches.

Kevin is standing over her.

She looks … dead.

Fear grips my insides like a vice. I can't draw breath from my lungs. It's as if they've stopped working. Oh my God … Elle. What has he done?

'Elle!' I scream, dropping the monitor to the floor.

I sprint from the room, down the stairs and rush to the basement door, but I can't open the damn padlock. I grasp for the key around my neck, my hands trembling so violently that I can't make them work.

I curse myself over and over as my stupid hands fumble with the deadbolt. I rush down the stairs and, in my haste, forget about the dodgy step, but somehow, I'm able to stop myself from tumbling to the bottom by grabbing the rail. My elbow smashes against the wall, but I barely notice the pain.

I shove the shelving unit aside and unlock the door, not bothering to knock.

'I swear to God, Kevin, if you've killed her, I'm going to kill you!' I shout as I fling the door open.

Kevin is now sitting on his bed, in his usual position, but Elle is on the floor. I can't tell if she's breathing from this distance. I rush to her side, kneeling to lean over her, listening and feeling for any signs of life.

There ...

A faint breath.

Thank God. She's alive.

She's ...

A fist to my face catches me completely off guard. Elle leaps to her feet, shoves me aside and sprints out the door.

'Elle!' I crawl towards the door, but it's too late. She slams it, leaving me sealed inside the prison of my own making, with my twin brother who I put there.

24

Kevin
Three Hours Ago

Twenty years ago, my beloved twin sister murdered our parents and then locked me inside a sealed room in the basement of our home. It was supposed to be temporary, but the days passed one by one. They turned into weeks, which turned into months, which turned into years. Twenty. Long. Years.

I'm still here.

I'm not the same person who first entered the basement all that time ago. Day by day, week by week, month by month, year by year, my soul has degraded, leaving me empty of any sort of emotion. My strongest emotion, if I can even call it that, is my determination to escape. Or maybe my strongest emotion is the pure hatred I now feel towards my once-beloved twin sister, who has betrayed me from the start. I started out as feeling sorry for her, but that soon passed when she continued to keep me locked up like a prisoner. I want her to pay for what she's done to me.

I want her to die.

I want her to ... suffer.

The sad thing is, though, Vera thinks she's been protecting me. She thinks by keeping me hidden from the outside world, she's keeping me safe. She's convinced herself I'm dangerous, that if I ever got out, I'll do it again. I'll kill people. She's not wrong. I would kill someone if I had to in order to survive, even her. It's human nature. No one is born wanting to kill people. But even a normal, healthy person has no idea what they're capable of when faced with the choice between life and death.

The truth is that twenty years ago, I was a normal kid who just wanted to help and protect his sister. She was sick and our parents made her that way, but now, after so long being cooped up with nothing but a fucking mouse for company, I've changed too.

I'm sick. I can feel it. The pain increases every day, but I've never told Vera. She wouldn't believe me because I can't prove it, other than point out that I'm losing weight rapidly despite eating whatever she provides me. I must be deficient in a lot of vitamins and minerals despite her giving me multivitamin supplements – vitamin D, for example – but it's not that that's killing me. I'm not sure how much longer I have left, but I'm determined not to die in this room. I don't care what it takes. I will not die here. I will not be forgotten. I will not end up buried behind the fucking garage, decomposing along with my parents. I deserve better.

I'm not the same person I was twenty years ago. Back then, at the start, I had hope, but without hope, a person has nothing to live for. Perhaps that's why my body is dying – because I've not given it hope that it will be free one day. For a long time, I accepted my fate. I even had the belief that Vera would come through for me. She promised to keep me safe, which she did, even though I wasn't the one who needed protection, but it was better to let her believe I was the murderer rather than allow her to know the truth. I'd known she was unstable for a while.

It started when she was six. I found her standing beside my bed in the middle of the night. It scared the life out of me, but she didn't remember it the next day when I told her. I don't think it was sleepwalking. I didn't tell our parents, but it happened several times. One time, when we were teenagers, I found her standing out in the yard, staring at the sky, and she said, 'The sky is red today … like blood. It's so pretty.' She stood out there for about three hours before she came in, acting like nothing had happened.

The first time Vera was violent, during one of her weird staring episodes, I became afraid of my sister. She attacked me, ripped at my face with her fingernails, hit me with her fists, screamed and spat at me. She had no idea what she was doing, but the fire in her eyes was something I'd never seen before, nor did I see it again …

Until the night when everything changed.

That night of our sixteenth birthday.

When I finally emerged from my hiding place, after she'd told me to get out of her room, I found her standing in the middle of her bedroom over the bodies of our parents. I knew then that I had to make a difficult decision.

But ever since that night, what little belief and hope I had has slowly been extinguished. Little by little my soul has been destroyed, shrivelled up into nothing. Now, twenty years of solitude has warped my mind, and so has whatever vile disease that's eating away at my body.

My only wish is to see the sky again before I die. And now, finally, I have a chance.

Elle is my chance.

And I don't care what I have to do to that girl, she's my escape route.

She's a pretty little thing, delicate and seemingly innocent. The only women I've seen, other than my sister, are on the television screen. Seeing one in the flesh is like being in the presence of a magical unicorn. I was beginning to think maybe Vera and I were the only two people left on the planet, my mind coming up with all sorts of strange and unlikely scenarios.

Like I said, I'm not myself anymore.

Maybe I am dangerous.

I know it's a risk to attempt to escape this house. Vera has told me many times over the years that the police are after me for the murder of our parents, but I'm not sure I believe her. It's difficult to know what's the truth and what's a lie when it comes to her. She's an expert at making people believe whatever she wants them to believe. However, I do have one advantage: my anonymity.

No one has seen my face in twenty years. It's a strange yet empowering realisation, one that fills me with both dread and excitement. I'm invisible, for all intents and purposes. Therefore, I don't technically exist, especially on paper in the real world. I have no bank account, no tax number, no registered home address, no phone number and no passport or form of ID, not a current one anyway. I highly doubt Vera has kept my belongings.

The bottom line is that the people out there don't know

what I look like. Vera wouldn't have shown them a picture, not a recent one anyway, otherwise she'd be revealing that she'd seen me.

If I can escape, then I can hide in plain sight. I'm sure there are people out there who can create fake IDs or I can just steal someone else's identity. Granted, I have no real plan on how I'd accomplish that, but I'm sure I could steal someone's wallet easily enough and go from there.

However, Vera is now no longer the only person who knows of my existence ... Elle does too, but it shouldn't be too hard to keep her quiet. I'll ask nicely. We seem to have hit it off already. She doesn't even seem like she's afraid of me. Brave girl.

I wonder what it would take for her to be afraid of me. What would it take for her eyes to glaze over and for her to wet herself from fear? I doubt it would take much, but I must be careful. I need her to trust me, otherwise she won't help me. I'll deal with her afterwards, after I'm out.

I bet she wants to escape as much as I do. Actually, no, that's impossible. There's no way she could want to escape more than I do. She hasn't been locked in here for twenty years.

Elle's been staring at me for several minutes, her brain ticking over, assessing the situation. Even if I wanted to, I couldn't reach her to hurt her, so she probably feels relatively safe right now. Vera can't keep her locked in here with me forever. We both need to eat and drink and soon. Vera loves me. If she wanted me to die, she would have let me starve years ago. This girl may not be her flesh and blood, but something tells me that Vera cares about her more than she should for someone who isn't related to her. Vera has been starved of human contact just as much as I have. She's had no relationship, no family, no friends. Her life has been as empty as mine. I remember her always saying she wanted to have a daughter one day. Perhaps Elle has filled that particular void in her soul for a short time, but now things have spiralled out of control, and I expect Vera is losing all sense of direction.

But this girl ... she cares about this girl.

I can use that.

'Elle,' I say softly. 'We can help each other.'

She looks up at me, her dark blonde hair falling across her face. 'How?'

'Vera has that camera in here, but no sound. She cares about you.'

'What do you suggest?'

'Vera doesn't have eyes on this room all the time. See that little red light up there? That means it's on, but she's not watching the feed. When it turns green, that's when she's watching.'

'How do you know that?'

'I've been in here a long time. I know things. I know how her mind works. She'll have to feed us and give us something to drink at some point, but she'll be expecting you to put up a fight. You heard her earlier ... she needs time to think, which means she'll be putting contingency plans in place to make sure you don't get out. But I know Vera. She's overly emotional, especially when it comes to protecting someone she cares about. Look what she did to our parents to protect herself and me.'

Elle narrows her eyes at me. 'What are you getting at?'

'If you lie on the floor and pretend to be injured, then she'll rush in here to save you. She'll let her guard down.

Maybe she'll leave the door open. Then you can run and escape.'

Elle frowns. 'What about Vera? She'll come after me.'

'Not if you lock her in here with me.'

'What about you?'

'Vera has a key on her that will unlock these cuffs.'

'You're not going to hurt her, are you?'

'No, of course not. I will get the key off her somehow, then lock her up in here instead and call the police.'

'Do you think she'll go to prison?'

'I hope so,' I say a little harsher than I mean to.

Elle is quiet for a moment. What else can I say to make her trust me? Surely, she doesn't think I did actually murder my parents?

'You must believe that Vera is dangerous. Why else would she keep me locked down here? The woman's deluded. Always has been.'

Elle studies me. I hold eye contact with her. I wish I could tell what she's thinking.

'Okay,' she says. 'I'll do it.'

I try not to sigh with relief. 'Great. Now, to make it look real, you need to come closer, so it looks as if I've attacked you.'

Elle gulps. 'Do I have to?'

'I won't hurt you; I promise.'

Elle frowns at me and then slowly stands up.

I smile for the first time in twenty years. I notice Elle flinch at the sight of my rotten teeth. But I don't care.

I'm getting out of here. I'm free.

25

Elle

My ankle explodes in molten pain as I throw myself up the stairs after slamming the door, trapping Vera inside with her demented brother. They're both crazy. I don't trust either of them, which is why I have every intention of calling the police as soon as I can find a phone. I don't know how long it will take for Kevin to get the key from Vera, so I need to be as quick as possible.

Kevin may have acted like he has been the victim here, but there's something that doesn't sit right with me. He isn't as innocent as he tried to make out. I'm not sure what he's done, but I don't think Vera is safe. But I didn't have any choice but to trap her in there with him. He's chained to the wall. As long as she keeps her distance and doesn't give him the key, she'll be safe. Something tells me that she won't give him the key easily, no matter how good he is at persuasion.

Kevin thinks I've done this to help him escape, but there's no way I'm letting that happen. The police can find him locked up in that room and deal with him how they see fit. And Vera. I don't want any part of whatever happens to her. She deserves to be locked up for the rest of her life. I reach the basement door, stumble through it, then slam it shut and slide the deadbolt across.

I don't know where my phone is. In all the confusion, I've forgotten where I put it. Plus, it's useless at the moment ever since I dropped it in a puddle the other night. I can't see Vera's phone either. I've got no choice but to run into the village, but ...

There's a large dead body next to the front door. It's wrapped in numerous black bags. I don't need to see the person's face to know who it is.

My dad.

Vera's killed him.

I can't look away from the body-shaped bag. It's mesmerising.

Many emotions rage through me at once, but none of them is sadness. I don't care that my dad is dead because his death means I'm finally safe to go home. He can't hurt me anymore. Vera may be some sort of psychopath, and a murderer too, but she's saved me from him, and now I've just trapped her down in her own basement.

But I can't think about her. I have to save myself.

I fling open the front door and run across the yard, heading for the dark path that leads into the village. It's so dark. Even the moon is hidden behind thick clouds, making it impossible to see more than a few feet in front of me. The tall trees and bushes block out the night sky and I'm so disorientated that I'm not sure I'm even running in the right direction.

But I keep moving forwards.

Away from Dawn House.

Away from Vera, and Kevin, and my dad.

There's no jacket to stop the sharp branches slashing through the skin on my arms and legs, but I barely feel the sting. I just keep running on my injured ankle. But it's horribly weak and it doesn't take long before I catch myself on a divot in the path and face-plant the ground.

My hands fly out to stop myself, but I'm not fast enough. Mud splashes my face and enters my mouth as I cry out in pain, my ankle exploding with heat once more. I somehow drag myself to my feet, and limp along the path, still not completely convinced that I'm heading in the right direction.

But ten long and agonising minutes later, the lights from the village come into view. I don't remember seeing a police station, but all I need is a phone. If I can get myself to Laura's, I think, then she can help me. I don't know where Carl lives, or Stacey, so Laura is my only option.

I throw myself at the front door to her building and bash my fists against it, calling her name. She opens the door and lets out a small yelp when she sees me standing on her doorstep, covered in mud and blood, trembling from head to toe.

'What the actual hell?' she says, but she doesn't make any sort of move to let me inside.

Tears stream down my face. 'Police,' I splutter. 'I need to call the police.' I can barely move my mouth to form words.

She frowns at me. It looks as if she's in two minds whether to help me or not, but eventually she sighs and steps aside. 'Fine. Come in then but stand on the doormat until I can fetch a towel. I don't want you dripping all over my floor.'

I'M CAUGHT up in a whirlwind of questions, lights and more questions. Police officers, paramedics and half the village turn up and surround Laura's place. She flitters about, moaning and telling people off, but in a weird way I think she's enjoying the attention.

Hamilton jumps up on my lap and refuses to move. It's soothing to stroke his soft fur. It takes me three attempts before I'm able to explain what's happened to me. I tell the police about Vera, about Kevin, about my father and who I really am; Elle Walter. I have to repeat myself to at least four different people and I can feel what little strength I have waning. I'm so hungry and down several glasses of water, quenching my extreme thirst.

Laura eventually hands me a sweet cup of tea when the commotion has died down about four hours later, but honestly time seems to have melted away and I have no idea what the time actually is. Apparently, the media are on their way to get a story for the morning news. My mother has been informed of where I am, and I'll be returned to her soon once I've been questioned again at the police station in Gloucester.

'Here. Drink this,' says Laura.

She's been strangely nice to me throughout all of this. Maybe she feels sorry for me. I'm almost expecting her to say, 'I told you so,' but she doesn't. I take the cup from her, but don't take a sip. Instead, I stare down at the murky liquid, watching as steam swirls around the rim of the mug.

'Thank you,' I say. Hamilton raises his head from my lap and then settles back down when he realises there are no biscuits.

'So ... Elle ...' The way she says my name reminds me of when my mum used to tell me off. 'There's something you should know,' she adds. I look at her, waiting. 'The police have released more details about Eric and his accident and ... it looks like he was killed. Someone cut his throat and then shoved him into the meat grinder.'

I lower my head. I've known it all along that it wasn't an accident.

'Vera was seen on the CCTV footage entering the shop around the time the accident happened.'

Somehow, I knew she was responsible. I'm so conflicted. What Eric did to me was wrong on so many levels, but did he deserve to die?

'Also,' Laura continues. 'The police raided Dawn House a few hours ago, but they only found one person in the locked room in the basement.'

I blink several times, attempting to restart my muddled brain. Clearly, I must have misheard her. Suddenly, Eric's unfortunate demise is the least of my concerns.

'What? That's impossible.' I very clearly remember slamming the door shut on both of them.

Laura shakes her head. 'They also found your father's body where you said it was.'

'I told them about the hidden door. I locked Vera and her brother in there. They both have to be down there.'

'They only found one person ... and they were dead.'

'Who is it?' My heart plummets. 'Who's dead?'

26

Vera

Four Hours Earlier

How can I have been so stupid and careless? As Elle slams the door in my face, I catch a glimpse of a smirk across her face. She's outsmarted me. I fell for her twisted performance. She used my own caring nature against me and now I'm trapped in this room with my brother, who probably isn't feeling very caring towards me right now.

I bang my fists against the door over and over, even though I know it's useless. I built this room, updated it several times to ensure it was completely soundproof and escape-proof. I mainly slam on the door to let out my frustration and anger. When I stop, I lean my forehead against it and take a breath.

Then I have a lightbulb moment, and I laugh at my own

forgetfulness. Because I planned for this moment. Of course I did. Granted, I hadn't expected to be locked in here by a teenage girl. I'd expected Kevin to escape somehow and trap me. I made a contingency plan years ago.

'Stop laughing!' Kevin's voice fills the room, causing the walls to vibrate.

I turn around slowly and stare at him. I'm not even a little bit worried about being in here with him. He can't reach me. I know exactly how long his chain is.

'That was your idea, wasn't it? Elle would never have done that to me of her own free will. What did you say to her?' I ask.

'Does it matter?'

'Why would you tell her to lock me in here with you? How is that going to help you escape?'

Kevin doesn't respond. He just continues to stare at me with a blank expression, not blinking or anything. 'Do you realise what you've done by letting her out?' I continue.

'Yes. Do you?'

I laugh again and shake my head. 'You've ruined everything! I've worked my fingers to the bone for twenty years to keep you safe and this is how you repay me? How dare you!' My voice has risen several octaves, but he doesn't flinch.

'It was going to end sometime, Vera. How much longer could you have kept this going? You're cracking under the pressure. I can see it in your eyes. You're not well, dear sister.'

That's when I laugh. 'You underestimate me ... dear brother.'

Kevin follows my every movement as I take small steps towards him. I stop just out of his reach, because I know the exact length of his chain. I pull up my sleeve and shake out the silver bracelet on my wrist, revealing a silver key attached. Kevin's eyes widen. He thinks he can see his freedom, smell it, but he's wrong. He's never getting out of here and I'd rather see him dead than in prison. He's my brother. He wouldn't survive in jail.

I unhook the key from the bracelet and hold it up, allowing it to sparkle under the dim lightbulb. His eyes darken. I turn my back, pull back a corner of the padding on the door and reveal a keyhole. It's the first time I've had to use it, but I'm thankful to my past self for putting in this safety feature, just like I did with the basement door. I don't remember closing it when I ran down the stairs earlier to check on Elle. So she's either got out that way, or she's managed to squeeze herself out the small window and escaped into the yard.

This small key is an extra safety feature for the door. There's the main key and deadbolt on the outside, but this one inside was fitted for this exact reason: so that I could escape if I were trapped in here.

The police will be on their way soon, so I can't afford to stay in here for much longer. If Kevin wants to get out of this room so badly, then he can stay here and be apprehended by the cops. I've done everything for him, kept him safe all these years, fed him, clothed him, but he doesn't care. He's ruined everything by allowing Elle to escape. It's time to put my past where it truly belongs: behind me. I need to think about myself and I'm not going to prison for something my brother did twenty years ago. He killed our parents, not me. I was doing the public a favour by locking him up, but I have a sinking feeling that the jury won't see it that way. I'll be a monster in their eyes, no better than those real-life killers in true crime documentaries.

It's time I left Dawn House. This is what his actions have done. I've got no choice but to leave him.

A low laugh sounds from behind me as I step towards the door to unlock it. Kevin's laughing at me. It sends shivers up and down my spine.

'What's so funny, dear brother?' I ask, turning around on the spot. I'm expecting to see him where I last saw him, on the bed, but he's standing directly behind me.

That's impossible. The chain.

How could he reach that far across the room?

He's so close I can smell his pungent breath on my face.

'Kevin,' I whisper.

I don't have time to react.

He moves like lightning as his hands reach up and grab me around the neck, squeezing tight. I cough and grasp his wrists, desperately attempting to loosen his grip. He's squeezing hard enough to immobilise me, but not enough to cut off my air supply; not yet anyway.

My eyes feel like they're about to burst. 'K-Kevin ... s-stop.'

'Do you know how long I've had to wait for an opportunity like this? Do you!' He grasps my hair and drags me away from the door, then kicks me in the ribs. I gasp for breath, both winded from the kick and desperately gulping in air after my windpipe was restricted. The dirty mattress breaks my fall as I stumble against the bed, but I catch my leg on a piece of metal sticking out from the side. It looks as if it's been bent and snapped off, but where's the missing piece?

That's when I see the end of the chain. The cuff is still around his ankle, but the end of the chain where it's supposed to be attached to the wall is no longer attached. The metal ring the chain is connected to has been pulled off the wall. It can't be possible, yet it's right there in front of my eyes.

'H-How?'

'Does it even matter to you how I did it?' he answers with an evil grin.

My body automatically shudders as I shuffle away from Kevin. He's moving towards me, and that's when I notice he's holding something in his dirty hand.

The piece of metal from the bedframe. It's small, but sharp; a perfect weapon. How could I have been so blind? He's been biding his time, waiting for me to slip up, waiting for any sort of opportunity to arise, and I gave him one on a platter. I threw a young girl into the room with him, opening myself up to being taken advantage of. That's exactly what's happened. He and Elle have taken advantage of me. I could have fixed this. I could have kept them both safe.

'Please don't do this, Kevin.'

Kevin lunges forwards, shoving the sharp piece of metal against my throat. He's stronger than he looks, and his odour is enough to turn my stomach.

'It's too late to beg, Vera. I begged you for years to let me out of this hellhole, and did you ever do it? Did you!' His shouts echo around the small room and I close my eyes against the force of his anger.

'You won't hurt me,' I say, my voice quivering. 'I'm your twin sister.'

'Twenty years ago, I wouldn't have hurt you, but a hell of a lot has changed since then, hasn't it? You're dangerous, Vera, and dangerous people deserve to die.'

I shriek as I kick him hard in the stomach. I don't have a plan. I just know I need to get out of here as soon as possible. He goes down hard to the floor, doubling over and groaning in pain, but as I leap past him towards the door, he grabs my ankle and yanks me on top of him.

We fight like cats and dogs, like we used to when we were kids. I remember rolling around on the playroom floor, kicking and biting like animals. Our mother had to pry us apart, but there's no one here to stop us this time. It's a matter of life and death. I've done this to him. I've created a monster by keeping him locked up and now he's a danger to society. I have to kill him. What if he gets out and goes after Elle? She's innocent in all of this and it's my fault she's wrapped up in it. I can't let him hurt her.

Kevin lets out a violent scream as he kicks me again. I do what I can, but I can already feel it's not enough. He has years of pent-up aggression pulsing through his body, the idea of freedom overwhelming all his senses so that he can't see anything else. Nothing else matters to him. Not me. Not Elle.

That's when I feel a blinding heat as the shard of metal slides into my side. At first, my brain doesn't register what's happened. Kevin lowers his face to mine, clutching the shard tight as he shoves it in deeper.

'It's kind of poetic, isn't it?' he says through gritted teeth. 'All this time, I thought I was the one who was going to die in this room, when actually ... it's you who gets that honour.'

My eyelids blink rapidly as I gasp and my body slides to the floor, my strength and blood flowing out faster every second. The heat spreads all around me, yet I feel so cold, as if my blood has turned to ice in my veins.

'I ... I was going to let you out,' I mumble. It's a lie. I don't know why I feel the need to plead for my life when I know it's going to end very soon.

Kevin shakes his head. 'By the time you did, it would have been too late.'

'What do you mean?'

'I'm dying, Vera. I can feel something eating me from the inside out.'

'I-I would have taken you to a doctor.' Another lie.

Kevin laughs. 'No, you wouldn't. You wanted me to die in this room one way or another.'

I'm lying on my back on the floor now with barely enough strength to keep my eyes open, but I must – if they close, I know it's over.

'P-Please,' I say. 'Help m-me.'

'I am helping you, dear sister.' Kevin slowly pushes the shard in deeper and a hot gush of blood escapes with it.

Kevin stands over me as my eyes close for the last time.

I can't help but think in that moment of Elle. I hope she's okay.

As I slip into darkness, the last image in my mind is of her.

27

Kevin

My dear sister should have died much more slowly. I should have left her in that room to die of dehydration and starvation, but I couldn't risk her being found by the police. I didn't want her to go to prison and have a chance to persuade people that she'd been the victim all along.

I don't have time to stop and enjoy the moment.

Vera dying without knowing how I fooled her makes me feel powerful. She had no idea of the lengths I've gone to over the years. It's surprising what time and perseverance can accomplish. Well, that and a digging utensil.

A plastic spoon to be more precise.

Three years ago, Vera fed me a dinner of soup, but when she collected the tray, the plastic spoon was missing. I told her I never received a spoon and drank the soup from the bowl. I don't think she believed me because she searched high and low for the spoon, even running her hands over my body, but she never found it. She gave up and admitted that she must have forgotten the spoon.

It was somewhere she'd never want or think to look. A man who is desperate to escape will do just about anything, even sticking a spoon up an orifice.

She'd never got close enough to check the chains in person, but she always glanced at the attachment on the wall. She would have never seen any sign of the concrete being worn away because I'd cleverly disguised it.

The cops will arrive and start tearing this place apart soon. So, as soon as her eyes close, I reach down and pull the thin chain from around her neck, snapping it with ease. There are several keys on the chain, and I'm not sure what keys unlock what door, but it won't hurt to take them all with me.

I also bend down, pulling the cuff of her top up to reveal the silver bracelet I gave her on our sixteenth birthday. I've noticed her wearing it every day, which surprises me. A sentimental artifact perhaps of a happier time, although I'd hardly have called our childhood a happy one.

I unclip the bracelet. She never knew the true story behind it and now she never will.

It takes a few attempts to find the correct key on the chain to unlock my ankle cuff. The relief is instant, and I sigh with pleasure as the metal ceases to rub against my sore, blistered skin.

I stand and head to the door, using the small key on the bracelet to open it. All these years, and I never realised she'd attached a small key to it to open the basement door from the inside. As it swings open, it stops short, catching on the shelving unit outside.

I know I need to move fast, but my body refuses to step foot outside the room. As much as I hate to admit it, I know I'm safe here. I have no idea what awaits me. Maybe Vera has been telling the truth and the police are after me for the murder of our parents, but that could be a lie. I won't know until I try.

Holding my breath, I place one foot over the threshold, followed by the other. Terror floods my body as I step outside of the room for the first time in two decades. I stand for a few seconds, debating whether she may have placed traps out here for me, taking note of my surroundings as I reassure myself that nothing bad is going to happen. The basement looks the same as I remember. I don't know what's out here. All the information I have is from BBC documentaries, films and sometimes news broadcasts. Vera didn't let me watch the news very often.

Technology has evolved, social media has exploded and then there was the pandemic that spread across the globe a few years ago. Vera and I were safe. We never contracted it, but I'm not protected by the vaccine, so who knows if I'm at risk. Is it still spreading? Am I in danger of contracting the virus and dying that way? My immune system is severely weakened, so the chances of me catching something must be pretty high. Now, I wonder if leaving my room, my place of safety is such a good idea.

But I know I can't think about it too much now. My main thought is of escaping and getting as far away from here as possible. But also, Elle. Should I have allowed her to escape? Maybe I was too hasty in my decision. I hadn't thought clearly about the repercussions of her escape. I'd never envisioned having someone else to think about when it came to me getting out of here. But now I realise that Elle knows what I look like. She's going to tell people about me, but if I'm not in that room when the police arrive, then I should be safe. Maybe they'll give up searching for me and say she's just a kid who's making up weird stories about being trapped in a basement by a crazy lady. Or maybe they simply won't understand why I would ever come after her.

In any case, I need to find her. I need to make sure she doesn't talk.

My weak legs shake as I ascend the stairs. The wonky step trips me up and I grab the rail to stop from falling.

'Still not fixed that fucking step,' I mutter.

I unlock the closed door. The bright light of the hallway makes me squint, but as my eyes adjust, I barely recognise the house. It's changed so much and not in a good way. The place looks like it's aged about a hundred years. The paint is peeling from the walls, the carpets are threadbare and the sideboards are covered in a thick layer of dust.

I scan the area. I don't know what I'm looking for, but it doesn't take long before I notice the body lying by the front door wrapped in black bags.

'Oh, Vera ... What have you done?'

I'm too late. She's killed someone else. Who is this guy? I kneel next to him and pull back some of the bags, searching his pockets. I pull out a leather wallet and look at the ID, a trick I learned from a TV show.

Nicholas Walter.

The name means nothing to me.

There is some money in the wallet, which I place in my pocket, along with a debit card. It may come in handy. I also pocket the ID. Stealing someone's identity for a while might be easier than I thought. There's also a grainy picture, curling at the corners, of a young girl in the wallet. It's Elle. A younger version, but it's Elle for sure, so that must mean this is her father. I have no idea why she's been staying with Vera and not living at home. It's a mystery I don't have time to dwell on. However, as I stand up and survey the scene, an idea pops into my head.

Perhaps Elle will run back home after she's spoken to the police. So, to find her, I need to know where she lives. But how do I find that out?

My mind is telling me to get out of the house now, but there are things I need to do first. Maybe there's a clue as to Elle's address in the room she's been staying in. I'm not sure which room it is, but it's worth a shot. I also need a change of clothes, something to disguise the fact I've been fermenting in my own filth for twenty years.

Before I know it, I'm at the top of the stairs, looking at the door to Vera's room. Her old bedroom is behind me. The room where it happened. The door is locked, so I fumble around with the keys on the chain until I find the right one. I push the door open. It's almost the same as I remember. She hasn't changed anything except for the design of the bedding. I'm not sure why I want to set eyes on where it happened. Closure, perhaps.

There's nothing in here for me, so I turn and enter her new bedroom. I'm not surprised she decided to sleep in a different room. Who'd want to sleep in the room where they murdered their own parents? Curiosity overrules everything else. I step into the room and begin to search through her things, including the wardrobe where I find some old clothes of Dad's, which I exchange for my dirty ones. It's not that I've enjoyed living in my own filth and refusing to wash; I just didn't see the point, but now I'm about to head outside where there are actual people, I can't walk around looking like a homeless person.

I catch a glimpse of myself in the wall mirror and do a double take. Bloody hell. I look old. Twenty years ago, I was a teenager yet now I could pass for a fifty-year-old, rather than my thirty-six years. I don't have time to sort my appearance out, but I will have to at some point. Not that anyone knows what I look like, apart from Elle, but if I wander around looking like a walking corpse then I'll be noticed for all the wrong reasons.

I turn and grab my old clothes, stuffing them into a bag I find in Vera's wardrobe. I can't leave any evidence that I was here. I head up to the next floor, searching each room for any sign a teenage girl was staying there.

I finally reach the attic room and do a quick search, but Elle doesn't have many possessions, so I traipse downstairs, muttering my annoyance. My rumbling belly leads me to the kitchen and that's when I see it; a backpack on the floor by the back door. It's not something I can see Vera using, so it must belong to Elle.

I shove a few mouthfuls of leftover food from the kitchen table into my mouth and down a glass of water before rushing to the backpack and turning it upside down. A few more pound coins, an old chocolate bar and a change of clothes. The backpack has seen better days. She must have used it every day. A small, worn label, which is sewn into underside of the flap at the top, catches my eye.

It says, 'This belongs to Elle Walter. If found, please return to 26 Elm Drive, Gloucester.'

Bingo.

After memorising the address, I sidestep the body of the

poor unfortunate soul who decided to enter Vera's domain and open the door to the outside world. It may be dark, but the fresh air is like a tidal wave of pure oxygen. I gasp and take several moments to compose myself, waiting for my weak lungs to adjust. I haven't breathed in clean, fresh air for so long, it's like they've forgotten how to work properly.

I have no idea where I'm going, or how I'm going to get there, having only the cash and debit card I found in the wallet to get me by. All I know is that I must find Elle. I have to put a stop to her story about the man she was locked up in a basement with.

As far as the world knows, Kevin Marks doesn't exist.

And I intend to keep it that way.

28

Elle

Laura tells me that Vera was found dead in the basement room, but there was no one else there. My own body won't stop shaking from the shock of finding out Vera is dead, and Kevin has managed to escape. Yes, the plan for him was to escape after I'd run away, but why? Why was he so determined to stay away from the police?

I didn't mean for Vera to die. I didn't think he'd kill her. He said he wouldn't. I shouldn't have trusted him, but I didn't have a choice. I had to get out of there. Clearly, he's unpredictable and violent – and he is now out there running riot. What have I done? Was he telling the truth about Vera killing their parents, or was it him all along? Am I now in danger?

Maybe they're both dangerous. Either way, it doesn't

matter because Vera is dead, and Kevin is on the loose. I explain everything to the police that Kevin told me, including how Vera killed their parents.

I tell them as much as I can about Kevin, about Vera and anything else I can think of, including the fact that Kevin admitted he and Vera had buried their parents behind the garage. They record me, and they write stuff down in their little notebooks, nodding their heads.

'How did Vera die?' I ask.

'It appears she was stabbed in the side with a sharp piece of metal that looks as if it had been broken from the bed,' replies the female officer, who has short, black hair. 'Kevin then must have taken the key from Vera and unlocked his cuffs, but there's also evidence of the chain being free from the wall. It looks as if he'd spent a long time digging away the concrete, then replacing it with bits of food so Vera didn't notice.'

I raise my eyebrows, quite amazed at the lengths he has gone to. 'What did he do with the bits of concrete he took from the wall?'

'It's possible he ate them over time as there's no evidence of them anywhere.'

Laura is sitting next to me, supposedly for moral support, but she hasn't said anything in a while. I know she's only here for the gossip; it has nothing to do with making me feel better.

The police officer stands up and puts away her notebook. 'I think that's all the questions we have for you at present. In the meantime, we have contacted your mother and she is expecting to meet you at the police station where you'll write your statement. We'll be in touch with any further questions in the next few days once the bodies have been exhumed.'

I look up. 'What about Kevin? Are you going to search for him?'

'Yes, we are. At the police station, we'd like you to describe him in as much detail as possible for our forensic sketch artist. We have a search team in the area.'

I stare open-mouthed at the police officer. 'What about me?'

The police officer stares back. 'What about you?'

'What if he comes after me? Can't I have some sort of police escort or something?'

'Do you believe you're in danger?'

'Yes!'

'Why do you think that, Elle?'

'Because I'm the only person who knows what he looks like, and he knows I will have told you all about him.'

'But, according to your statement just now, he allowed you to escape, and it was your plan to lock him in the room with Vera.'

'Y-Yes, but ...' I have no words left. I can't explain it. I just know he's after me, it's like a gut feeling. But it's clear that whatever I say to the police won't be taken all that seriously. Because they are right; I don't have proof Kevin will come after me. Just a feeling.

Maybe the officer feels sorry for me or maybe she notices how pale I've turned because she adds, 'Okay, how about once you're back at home with your mum, I send a patrol car round once in a while to check up on you, yeah?'

I give her a small nod in thanks. I'd rather have armed police patrolling my house at all hours of the day and night, but I guess the police force aren't rolling in spare cash for that sort of thing.

'Do I have to go home to my mum?' I ask, glancing sideways at Laura who avoids my gaze. She's probably hoping I don't ask to stay here with her.

'Well, you're still underage, Elle. Do you not want to return home?'

'I guess the reason I ran away in the first place is now gone, so ...'

The officer nods, as if understanding. 'Your father. Did he abuse you?'

I nod again, my head hanging forwards, almost touching my chest. 'You could say that,' I mumble.

'Did your mother know about it?'

This is a conversation I really don't want to be having right now. 'I don't know.'

The officer nods and clears her throat. 'Right. I see. We'll be speaking with your mother about this too when she arrives at the station.' She takes a deep breath and holds it, then exhales as she says, 'We'll be off then. Elle, as I said, you can expect a visit from the police within the next few days at your house. An officer will be along in a minute to collect you and drive you to the station in Gloucester where your mum will meet you.' Then she walks out of the room, along with the male cop who has barely said a word, leaving me alone with Laura.

I busy myself by stroking Hamilton, enjoying the feel of his tiny heartbeat against the top of my thigh. Laura stands up and paces up and down in front of me.

'There's something else you should know, Elle,' she finally says. 'About Eric.'

At this I look up, frowning. 'What about him?'

'The cops didn't want to question you about it now as it's not really connected to this case, but ... well ... Vera wasn't the only person who had means and motive to kill him.'

'Huh?'

'You were seen at the pub the other night with him and apparently you argued and stormed out. He was really upset over it. He said the next morning that you ... you got drunk and accused him of raping you, causing a scene when he tried to calm you down.'

My mouth falls open and I stop stroking Hamilton, which makes him whine quietly. 'W-What? I never ... I never said that. He didn't ... I mean ...' I take a deep breath, trying to find the right words. 'He didn't rape me, but he did drug me. Well, not with drugs, but with alcohol. I'd never drank alcohol before, and he put vodka in my drink without me knowing.'

Laura lowers her eyes to the floor. 'Eric is a lovely boy. I've known him since he was a baby.'

'And what, because I'm new in town, you think I'd just make up random stories for fun?'

Laura sighs and stands up. 'I don't know what to tell you, Elle. But Eric isn't like that.'

'Maybe you should have asked him about Willow,' I snap before I realise what I'm saying.

Laura's face turns red. 'What do you mean?'

'Nothing. Forget it.'

'No. Go on. You think Eric had something to do with Willow's disappearance. Is that it?'

'They were dating, weren't they?'

Laura nods. 'Yes, and he was questioned at the time and for a while he was the main suspect, but there was no evidence to suggest foul play.'

'That's not what Vera thinks.'

'And you believe the word of a woman who kept her brother locked in a basement for twenty years, do you? And who locked you in there with him. Get a grip. The boy is dead. Vera killed him. Maybe you helped her out, I don't know, but if you ask me, you're the reason all this shit started. Ever since you came to town, things have gone wrong, haven't they?'

I clench my jaw and look away as tears fill my eyes. I'm annoyed at myself for allowing people to rile me up. I have so much more I want to say, but what's the point? Laura doesn't deserve my tears or my attention any longer.

I sigh as I stand up, sliding Hamilton off my lap. He gives me a lick to say goodbye.

I walk to the door and open it, then turn and look at Laura. 'Thanks for giving me a place to stay when I needed it.' And I walk out.

A police officer stops me as I step outside and tells me that a car is waiting to take me to Gloucester. I guess this is it. I'm going back home. I've only been here a few weeks, but it feels as if I've really settled in, although it's now clear that no one wants me here. Perhaps it's only Laura who feels that way, but I think I've overstayed my welcome. I hope Carl understands about me leaving so suddenly.

This isn't how it was supposed to turn out. This was supposed to be the start of my new life. Although, I have to admit that the thought of going back home is somewhat more appealing now than before when my dad was alive. My mum is the only family I have left and even though she could have stood up for me more, and made different choices, I should give her another chance. She was controlled by my dad as well and now she has a second chance too.

For a strange moment, I imagine Vera in a similar situation. She must have loved her brother deep down, right?

That's why she did what she did. Because she was afraid of losing him. He was mistreated by their parents too. Maybe not on the same scale as she was, but once her abusers were out of the way, she believed she had to keep him safe.

That's what I have to do for my mum now. She's never been the best parent, but ... she's all I have left.

Tears fill my eyes as I take a seat in the police car. Despite everything she's done, I miss Vera. She felt more like a mother to me than my own ever did, and now she's gone, and it's all my fault.

I look out at the dreary darkness. The two police officers in the front seats don't talk to me during the drive. I close my eyes for a moment and think back to my time in the basement room with Kevin. I'd only been in there a matter of hours, during most of which I was unconscious. God only knows how desperate he must have been by the end. A shell of his former self. Isolation does bad stuff to people. He won't know where to go or what to do, but he'll want to fixate on something on the outside. Me. I'm still certain he'll come after me.

'What's going to happen to all my stuff that I left at the house? I had a backpack,' I ask, after spending at least twenty minutes in silence.

'It will be bagged and returned to you once it's been checked over,' replies the officer who's driving.

'Checked over?' I ask. 'What are you looking for?'

The officer in the passenger seat turns and looks over his shoulder at me. 'Nothing for you to worry about. It's all just procedure. We'll be at the station soon.'

I blink twice. 'Do I have to go to the station? Can't you take me home first?'

'No, not yet. We need to take you into the station to ask

some more detailed questions, collect samples and take a written statement.'

'Samples? Samples of what, exactly?'

'Your DNA. All routine stuff, don't worry.'

'Am I under arrest or something?'

'No, not at all. It's just procedure.'

I lean my head against the car seat. 'Right. You said that.'

'Your mother is meeting us there.'

'Great,' I mutter. 'Has she been told about my dad?'

'I believe so, yes.'

'What did she say?'

'She asked if you were safe,' he said, then paused before adding, 'and whether you were the one who killed him.'

I scoff. Trust my mum to suspect me of murder as well. I don't say anything for the rest of the journey but focus on controlling my breathing. So much has happened, and my mind is frazzled with all the information and unanswered questions.

It takes a further twenty minutes to drive into Gloucester and then I'm led into the station, where I'm taken into a small, grey room, asked if I'd like anything to drink and then left alone.

I'm so tired I just want to close my eyes and sleep, but my body is still pulsing with adrenaline and anxiety. I twirl my hair round and round my fingers, yanking on the strands until I feel that satisfying snap. A female officer has already been in and taken a DNA sample from my mouth. She even asked if I'd been raped or sexually assaulted in any way. I told her no. I told her I didn't know why Eric had told people I'd said that, but it wasn't true. I did tell her about him spiking my drink, though. She made a note and said she'd investigate it. But since he's now dead, I guess the problem is moot.

It's not long before the door opens and my mum walks in, looking pale and thin. She's always seemed frail. I suppose it's because of what my dad put her through. She rushes forwards and wraps her arms around me before I even have the chance to rise from the metal chair I've been sitting in for the past hour. I hug her back, squeezing tight. I think this is the first time she's ever hugged me as a teenager. It feels odd and I'm not quite sure how I should feel about it.

'Are you okay?' she asks.

'I'm fine, Mum.'

'Where have you been? I was so worried.' Somehow, I'm not sure I believe her.

'I couldn't stay at home any longer. I'm sorry. I had to leave. I didn't want to end up like you.' I lower my head, afraid to look her in the eye. She touches my chin and slowly raises it, so I have no other choice but to look at her.

'No, I'm the one who should be sorry. And I am. I'm so sorry that I never did anything to stop your father. I was so afraid. I just thought that if I didn't say or do anything, it wouldn't be so bad.'

I want to scream at her. She's my mum. She should protect me, no matter what. Vera only knew me for a couple of weeks, and after I told her what Eric did to me, she made him pay. How could a woman I barely knew want to protect me more than my own mother?

I don't know why I keep trying to defend Vera's actions, but even though she was wrong, I'm sure that her heart was in the right place.

'What happened?' she asks me before taking a seat in the other chair next to me.

'I don't want to talk about it right now, Mum.'

'Y-You were living with a woman?'

'Yes.'

'And she killed your father?'

'Yes.'

Mum strokes my hair. 'Then we're safe now. Once we've got all this straightened out, we can go home. I know I haven't been the best mother to you, Elle, but I promise I'll do my best from now on.'

I want to believe her. I really do. I can only hope that we can get our relationship back on track after everything that's happened.

'Mum, he's out there,' I say.

'Who?' She looks confused, casting a nervous glance around her. 'Your father? He's dead, Elle. He can't hurt you anymore.'

'No, not Dad. Kevin. The man who was locked in Vera's basement. He escaped and I'm worried he might come after me. I'm the only person who knows what he looks like. He's dangerous and unstable. He has nothing to lose.'

'Why do you think that?'

'Isn't that how you'd be after being locked in a window-less room for twenty years?'

My mum nods slowly. 'I'm sure the police will find him, baby. You've got nothing to worry about. The police have told me that they're sending an officer round to check on us once in a while.'

I screw up my nose in response. What does once in a while mean? Once a day? Once a week? Kevin could be tracking me down right now.

'Have the police said anything else?' I ask.

My mum looks away, as if she'd rather be anywhere else

but next to me. 'I ... may have overheard something on the police radio earlier.'

'What?'

'They said they've found other bodies at that woman's house.'

Other bodies? Do they mean Vera and Kevin's parents? There are already four bodies at Dawn House: Vera, my dad, and Vera and Kevin's parents. Surely, there isn't another one?

'What? That makes no sense. Who?' My mum doesn't reply. I have to bite my tongue to stop from screaming at her. 'Mum!' I not-quite-shout. 'How many other bodies have been found?'

Tears fill her eyes and she staggers to her feet, edging towards the door. 'I ... I think I should get one of the police officers to explain. I ... I can't ...' She retreats out the door and slams it behind her, leaving me with my mouth open.

29

Kevin

Five Years Ago

Fifteen years is a long time. It's a long time to be alone with your thoughts. It's even longer when you're trapped in a room only ten foot by ten foot with nothing to occupy your mind other than the sweet release of escape. At first, I went along with Vera's harebrained plan of keeping me hidden because I was afraid of her cracking at the seams. She's very unstable, so I played the good brother and kept quiet, but as the years went by, I realised one thing; I'm never getting out of here unless I do something about it.

That's when I started using the plastic spoon I'd stolen to dig away at the concrete surrounding the metal ring lodged into the wall. The soundproofing padding makes it awkward to reach, but on the other hand it helps to cover up the loose concrete. However, not for long. I have to eat some of the concrete to hide it from Vera, which is not a pleasant experience on the way in or the way out.

I'm lying on my side on my bed with my knees pulled up to my chest, groaning in pain when Vera knocks on the door and then enters. I don't sit up against the wall like normal because my insides feel like they are rotting. Perhaps that last piece of concrete was a little too big for my body to process.

'What's wrong?' she asks from the doorway.

'Nothing,' I mutter, avoiding her gaze, but something catches my eye, so I turn my head and look at her. She's sweating, her hands covered in dirt. Her welly boots are also muddy. 'What have you been up to?'

'Nothing,' she echoes.

'It doesn't look like you've been doing nothing.'

She huffs at me the way our mum used to when we'd get on her nerves by asking loads of questions. 'Do you want your lunch or not?'

'No, I don't.'

'Why not?'

'My stomach hurts.'

Vera sighs. She's always had a soft spot for me when I'm unwell. Several years ago, I contracted a bad infection and needed antibiotics, which she somehow got for me. But she hasn't been near me for a long time, ever since I attacked her. I guess I can't blame her, but her caring nature is still there under the surface. I can't say the same about mine. If I had half a chance, I'd slit her throat from ear to ear.

'Do you need painkillers?' she asks.

'Yes. Lots.'

'You can have the appropriate amount. I'll be back soon.'

She closes the door and leaves me to my slow death. When she appears ten minutes later, I notice she's washed her hands and changed her footwear. She places a plastic cup of water on the trolley and two white pills before pushing it across the floor towards me. I sit up and take the pills and drink the water. I may not be hungry right now, but I won't pass on the opportunity to stay hydrated.

'Were you gardening or something?' I ask, placing the empty cup back on the trolley.

'No.'

'Then why were you covered in dirt?'

'Enough questions.' She turns to leave.

'Wait!' She stops and turns to look over her shoulder at me. 'Vera ... please ...' I'm not sure why I'm begging. Maybe it's because I'm in pain and worried I might die because a piece of concrete is lodged in my stomach or intestinal tract, or maybe I'm just so tired of being in this room.

'I'll check on you later,' she says and then closes the door.

I cry like a baby, curling back up into a foetal position, but the painkillers do their job and I'm able to fall asleep. When I wake up the pain is less. I use the bucket in the corner successfully. I think I'm out of the danger zone. No more eating concrete for a while. My escape plan will have to be put on hold. There's no point in killing myself.

Then I think of Vera and how she acted earlier. She was dripping in sweat and filthy. She'd been doing something, but what? The only thing I can think of that makes sense is that she's dug up our parents' bodies and moved them, but why? Are the police sniffing around? Are they suspicious for some reason? Is she worried about being found out?

As I lie on my bed, staring at the ceiling, my mind goes

round and round in circles. I focus on steadying my breath and composing myself. I've had many a panic attack in this room. How will I react when I'm finally faced with the outside world? What will it be like?

What will I do when I get out? These questions and a dozen more like them keep me awake for the rest of the day. Vera brings me dinner at six o'clock and I manage to eat a small amount. She's showered and changed, but there's something behind her eyes that fills me with worry.

Something's happened outside of this room.

The question is: what has Vera done now?

30

Elle

The same female police officer I saw earlier comes in several minutes later and asks me to take a seat, pointing to it as if she thinks I haven't noticed it's in here. All my body wants to do is move; I don't feel like sitting down. It feels better to keep pacing up and down the small room, but she stares at me until I'm forced to sit. She nods and takes a seat opposite me. My legs keep twitching and I continuously fiddle with my hair as she talks to me in a soothing voice, but the tone sounds patronising, like she's addressing a young child.

'I thought you'd like to be kept up to date with our investigation,' she says. 'The area behind the garage at Dawn House has been thoroughly searched. The remains of a grown man and a woman have been found. They appear to have been buried for approximately twenty years, which matches the time of their disappearance.'

I nod, already knowing all of this.

'Those remains, along with the corpses of Vera herself and that of your father make four in total. However, we also deployed a trained cadaver dog in the grounds of Dawn House. They found a fifth body buried in the front garden, under a rose bush. Forensic examination confirmed it as the body of a young woman, approximately eighteen to twenty years of age.'

I hear what she says, but the words don't make sense. A young woman buried in the front garden. How is that possible? But then her meaning clicks into place. Willow. It has to be, and it must be that Eric buried her there five years ago. That's why he was always so interested in Vera and her house and why he kept asking me all those questions about me moving in with her.

'Who is it?' I ask, even though I know.

The police officer shifts in her seat. 'We won't know that until the DNA has been tested. The body of the young woman was buried much later than the other two behind the garage. Several years later, in fact. It's likely that the woman has only been there a few years. Six at most. We do have an idea as to who it could be.'

'It's Willow Baxter, isn't it?'

'I'm afraid I can't say until the results of the DNA tests come back.' I sense her gaze on me, scrutinising me. 'Are you okay? You've turned very pale.'

I reach forwards and take the plastic cup of water from the table. 'Yes, I'm fine. What about the basement room?'

'What about it?'

'I mean, is there any other DNA down there other than Kevin's and Vera's?'

'Other than yours, no. It doesn't appear as if anyone else has been inside that room.'

'Have you found Kevin yet?'

'Not yet. Once you've provided a detailed description to our sketch artists then we'll have more to go on. However, we can't confirm if he poses a threat to you. His sole focus will be on escaping. We don't believe you are at any risk.'

Panic floods my body. 'He is dangerous. I know he is.'

'To be honest, Elle, you were lucky to survive at all. Considering how unpredictable Vera was and given the number of bodies we've found, it seemed highly likely that she could have targeted you next. She's killed her parents, your father and Eric Porter. And possibly the young woman we found in the garden. Technically, that makes her a serial killer.'

'Vera wouldn't have hurt me,' I say without thinking. 'She cared about me.'

'Maybe so, but she wasn't well. There's no telling what she could have done. But she's no danger to you now.' The police officer smiles at me. 'Now, I'll send the sketch artist in and once you've spoken to her, you're free to go home with your mother. I'll come and visit you for a follow-up interview in a few days. How does that sound?'

I don't have the energy to keep repeating myself. I want to go home and hide in the basement for a while. I want to see Trevor.

TWO HOURS LATER, my mum holds the front door open and I walk through, not quite believing I'm back where I started, but now there's not the terror of knowing my dad is behind the door waiting for me. My mum drops my backpack on the floor just inside the front door. The police officers returned it after they'd searched through the items inside. Not that there was anything interesting in there.

'Can I get you anything?' my mum asks as the door clicks closed.

'No,' I reply. 'I think I'll just go to bed.' The idea of doing anything else is impossible. Even eating. My stomach is rumbling, but all I want to do is sleep.

But what happens when I wake up?

Do Mum and I act normal and pretend as if the past couple of weeks never happened and I didn't run away from home with a fake ID because I was sick and tired of living here with her and Dad?

Mum sighs as I walk up the stairs. When I get to the top step, I turn and look down at her. 'Mum ... what happens now?'

'We continue on with our lives, baby.'

'Dad's dead.'

'Yes, he is, but we'll be okay. I still have my job, and now you can do whatever you like, and I'll do my best to support you.'

'You mean I can go to university?'

Mum nods and smiles. 'Yes, if that's what you want to do. I won't hold you back from your dreams, Elle. I promise you I'll spend the rest of my life trying to make it up to you.'

The only thing I can do is smile. I don't know how I'm supposed to feel about this. Clearly, Mum feels guilty about the way she's acted over the years by not protecting me, but if I attend university, I'll be leaving her all alone. She has no friends, no family, no support network. Over the years, they've all left her because Dad caused such disruption whenever they visited and I doubt she'll be able to mend those burned bridges.

I leave Mum downstairs and head to my bedroom, locking the door. It's early morning, almost seven, and I'm so tired I can barely keep my eyes open. I kick off my trainers, crawl under my duvet and pull it up over my head, blocking out the light sneaking in through the curtains, which have been haphazardly drawn across the window.

Several minutes, or it could have been several hours later, a creaking sound wakes me from a deep but troubled sleep. When I peer out from behind the covers, I can't see anything in my room. It's dark. When did it get dark? Did I sleep all day and it's now the following night?

The creaking sound appears again from the furthest corner of my room. If I were a kid, I'd be calling for my mum right about now, complaining of a monster hiding under my bed or something. But I'm not a child; I can control my imagination.

My eyes take a few seconds to adjust to the darkness, but eventually a shape emerges.

There's a man standing in the corner of my bedroom, hidden in shadows.

I scream.

Loud footsteps thud up the landing and my mum bangs on the bedroom door. As I sit up in bed and turn on my bedside light, I manage to stop screaming. As light floods the room, the man disappears.

'Elle! Open up!'

I scramble out of bed and unlock my door. 'I'm okay, Mum. Sorry. Bad dream.' She's in her dressing gown. 'What time is it?'

'Midnight. You've been asleep for almost seventeen hours. I thought it best just to let you sleep. I knocked for you several times, but you told me to come back later.'

'I did?'

'You don't remember?'

I shake my head. 'I must have been half asleep. I saw him, Mum. He was standing in the corner of my room just now.'

'Who?'

'Kevin, the man Vera kept in her basement.' Tears fill my eyes and my mum envelops me in a tight hug, stroking my hair. She looks at the corner of the room. There's nothing there, but I can't get the image out of my head that there was. Or could have been. I don't know what to believe anymore.

'We'll get to the bottom of this, I promise.' My mum's voice is calm, soothing, but her words do nothing to quell the anxiety swirling in my stomach.

Kevin's here. He must be.

How did he get inside my house?

It's impossible. Yet ... how can I trust my own mind after everything that's happened?

THE NEXT MORNING, while I'm forcing down a bowl of soggy Coco Pops, as if I'm five years old again, Mum's phone rings. She answers and immediately turns her back to me and lowers her voice, so I know it's about me. I don't bother to listen in but continue to watch the news broadcast. There's been no mention of Vera yet, but I'm expecting the story to break any day now.

'That was the police,' Mum says. 'They said the identity

of the dead girl they found in the garden is going to be announced today. Her family have been informed.'

I lower the spoon back into the bowl and stare at Mum, holding my breath.

'Shall I put the news on?'

I nod slowly, turning towards the television. I already know who it is, but I'm interested to see if Eric is a suspect or not. However, since he's dead, there's not a lot more information they can glean. My body shivers, yet I'm not cold.

'The body of a young woman has been found buried in the front garden of Dawn House, a property belonging to Vera Marks, who was found dead in her basement late last night. The body is that of Willow Baxter, who disappeared from the village of Barrow-on-the-Water five years ago.'

I gulp, the cereal in my mouth tasting like damp cardboard.

'Initial reports suggest that Willow was struck on the back of the head by a blunt object. At the time, her boyfriend, Eric Porter, was questioned about her disappearance. He told the police that they had argued, and she had run away along the river. Despite the body being buried at Dawn House, there is no direct evidence to suggest that Vera Marks is responsible for Willow's death. Eric Porter was killed by Miss Marks several days ago, but at present Eric Porter is the prime suspect in Willow's murder as he was seemingly the last person to see her alive. More on this story as it develops.'

'Elle? Are you okay?' Mum asks.

I breathe out a long sigh. 'Yes. Fine. I ...' My eyes catch movement at the window and my head snaps round to look, but there's nothing there except for the big oak tree blowing in the wind. I stand and pick up my bowl and spoon. 'I've lost my appetite,' I say quietly.

31

Kevin

As I disappear down an overgrown path next to Dawn House, I hear sirens in the distance. It sounds as if I'm leaving at the right time. It didn't take Elle long to get to town and blab to the cops. My lungs burn and feel as if they might burst from the exertion of running. Being cooped up inside a room, attached to a length of chain for twenty years has severely weakened my lung capacity and overall fitness level.

But I cannot stop.

I need to get as far away from this village as quickly as possible. The cops will be swarming the area looking for me. They still have no idea what I look like, and I intend to keep it that way. It's why I have to find Elle. She's the only one who can destroy my freedom.

I'm not sure how long I run for before my legs collapse

beneath me and I land in a heap, splashing down in a muddy puddle. The rain is pouring down and I'm soaked through. My long, matted hair clings to my face, blocking my vision. I need to find shelter so I can rest and make a solid plan of action.

I have a bit of cash which I took from Elle's dad, but that's it. I have her address, but no means of getting there or even knowing where its neighbourhood is. It's been a long time since I went to Gloucester. Twenty years ago. The roads may have changed. I don't even know which direction I've been running in.

After crossing a large field, almost waist-high with grass, I arrive at a run-down shack. Perhaps it's some sort of shed for animals or a storage hut. Whatever it is, it's shelter from the wind and rain. The door is locked tight, but the window next to it has been smashed, so I crawl through it, falling into the little building with a thud.

Slowly but surely, I catch my breath and rest, my hearing on high alert for any strange sounds or voices. There's the odd hoot of an owl and some rustling in the trees either caused by the wind or a nocturnal animal. I can't sleep. My body won't switch off. I'm so fucking cold my teeth are chattering and I keep biting the inside of my mouth.

As soon as it starts to get light, I make a move, heading towards a river, which I know runs through several towns and villages in the area. As soon as I reach it, I take a drink to quench my thirst and try and wash my face, hands and feet as much as possible. I should have grabbed the dead man's shoes, but I didn't think to do it at the time. My feet are cut and bleeding from running last night.

I have to keep on the move. I eat the chocolate bar I found in Elle's backpack and continue following the river, keeping away from paths in case I come across any walkers. I know I still look a state and no doubt the cops have alerted the area to be on the lookout for a man who appears to be homeless.

My feet have their own pulse by the time I stumble on a small holding. It looks like a sheep farm, but it's fairly quiet still so I slink around the side of the nearest barn and slip inside. It's an empty shearing shed. There's a farmer's jacket hung up on a peg, and – thank God! – some old worker boots, which I put on, sighing with relief despite them being a bit big. I then spy some shears.

I use them to chop away at my mangled hair and beard. There's no mirror around so I can't check out my handiwork. I can't imagine I look much better, but it's something. I scavenge the shed for some food, but there's nothing suitable, so I head back outside and leave the farm.

I come to a main road and see a green sign pointing to Gloucester. At least I know I'm going in the right direction now. I could try and catch a bus to the city but want to save the little money I have, so I move back from the road, hiding myself in the tree line, and I continue walking.

By the time I enter civilisation, it's getting dark again.

From what I can see, everything has changed so much in twenty years. I barely recognise the area I grew up in as a child. The roads are bigger and there are more of them. There are more people too. People everywhere. In cars. Walking. Cycling.

My palms sweat as I walk along the pavement towards the city centre. Despite dreaming of being free for so long, the reality is much scarier and more daunting than I ever thought. All these people are causing my heart rate to increase every time they look at me. Do they recognise me or are they just curious about my bedraggled appearance?

I barely recognise myself in the reflection of the shop windows I pass. I remember myself as the sixteen-year-old boy who went into that room. Now I'm a nearly forty-year-old man with hair that's been attacked by sheep shears. There's not a lot I can do about my pale skin and gaunt figure right now. I need food and water, which I manage to find fairly easily. It's shocking what people throw away in street bins. Half-eaten burgers and bottles of juice. I do have a little bit of money, but I can't risk entering shops in case someone clocks my presence.

I eat well on other people's leftovers and then find a deserted alleyway behind a restaurant where I set up camp for the night next to an overhang, which helps to keep the rain off.

I have Elle's address but have no idea where to find it. I have no phone and no map. Should I ask someone for directions? Or attempt to find my own way? It's too late to do anything now, so I decide to wait until morning. Now, with a half-full stomach, I manage to fall asleep, wedged up against the wall.

I'm woken by the sound of raised voices. It's still dark and the temperature has dropped significantly. I pull my jacket tighter and attempt to settle back down to sleep, but it's no use. The morning hustle and bustle of the city is too loud and distracting.

Plus, my stomach is growling at me again.

However long it is later, after I've found something for breakfast in another bin, I walk through the drizzling rain towards the main part of town. Every now and then I recognise a sign or a shop that was there twenty years ago, but most of it's all changed. In fact, most of the stores are coffee shops, hairdressers and restaurants.

I come across a store that sells maps and other touristy items, so I enter, grab a map of Gloucester and tuck it under my jacket before leaving the shop. No way am I wasting my money on a map. I used to shoplift as a kid, and it appears I still have the thief's quick sleight of hand.

Once I'm far enough away from the shop to be sure I haven't been followed, I take out the map and search for Elle's street, which takes a lot longer than I might have expected. Having never learned to read a map, I struggle to follow it and get lost several times throughout the day, but finally I find myself standing on the other side of the road from her house. In the shadow of a streetlight, I simply watch for a few minutes. There's a light on inside on the ground floor, but all the curtains are drawn. I wonder if Elle is asleep. Or maybe she's not even there.

How am I going to play this? How am I going to get close to Elle?

I'm not a killer. I'm not Vera, but captivity has changed me. I've tasted freedom and I'm not about to let some runaway teenager blab about me to the cops. I don't want to kill her, but if that's what I must do to keep her quiet, then so be it.

I take a deep breath and am about to step across the road when I notice a car parked outside her house. There's a man inside, sitting in the driver's seat. Is that a cop watching her house? Or is it a friend waiting for Elle?

I decide not to risk showing myself. Instead, I disappear like a puff of smoke into the darkness.

. . .

UNDER THE COVER of the night sky, I circle around the neighbourhood and manage to find a way into the back garden of Elle's house. All the lights are off inside, but the moon and streetlamps provide enough light to see the outlines of garden furniture, as well as the windows and doors of the building. It's a fairly old house, but in far better condition than Dawn House. A part of me wants to burn my old house down to the ground, so it can never come back to haunt me again. However, now it's crawling with cops, so that's not going to be an easy mission to accomplish any time soon.

I creep up to the back door and unlock it using the key I found on the body of Elle's father. I knew it would come in handy. I let myself in and creep across the kitchen floor. The house is silent. I glance at the clock on the wall and see it's ten minutes past midnight, although quite what day of the week it is, I have no idea.

Maybe Elle is asleep upstairs.

Should I go and surprise her or bide my time?

That's when a creak that sounds as loud as a gunshot echoes through the house. Someone is coming. My body tenses and I grab a nearby door handle, pull it open and find myself standing at the top of a flight of stairs leading to a dark basement.

I smile at the cruel irony as I descend the stairs.

32

Elle

She's all over the news. Every station is talking about Willow. There is an interview with Carl and he spends most of it in tears, but then turns angry at the end, saying he's glad Eric is dead after what he did to his beloved daughter. According to the never-ending news updates, Willow had a severe contusion at the back of her head that could have been the cause of her death. No other injuries were present other than some small cuts and bruises.

Despite knowing I should be more upset by what happened to this innocent young woman, I'm far more concerned with Kevin still being out there. An unmarked police car has been parked outside for a while, and the officer every so often does a walk around the house, but he doesn't stay for long. During the night, there's no one patrolling the area.

I keep jumping at every shadow and sudden noise. To be honest, I can't take it anymore. I need to escape somewhere safe and quiet.

I leave Mum to stare absentmindedly at the television screen and head down into the basement to visit Trevor. I can't keep living in fear. I must face my demons. My dad is gone. There's no need to hide down here ever again. It's time to say goodbye.

I scan my eyes across the dim room, as memories pop into my head of hiding down here throughout my childhood years. I can't find Trevor, so I pull out the shelving unit and squeeze myself behind it one last time.

A low creak from the opposite side of the room makes my breath catch in my throat.

I peer out from behind the unit and look across the room where there are piles of boxes covered with a dark sheet. It's so quiet that I can hear my heart beating wildly.

Another creak, this time above me.

'Elle ... are you down there?'

'Mum? Yeah, I'm here,' I answer, keeping my eyes firmly fixed on the boxes.

'The police are on their way over to ask you some questions,' comes my mum's loud voice from upstairs. 'I need to pop out for a bit. I'll be back as soon as I can. Don't talk to them without me, okay? Make them a cup of tea or something and wait for me to get back.'

'Okay, no problem.'

I continue to stare at the oddly shaped pile of boxes as I listen to my mum move about upstairs and then shut the front door.

I slowly let out my breath.

One of the boxes shifts slightly ...

'Hello, Elle ...'

My first response is to freeze. Then I open my mouth to scream ...

'If you make a sound then I promise it will be the last thing you ever do.' Kevin steps out from the shadows and stands up to his full height. His long hair and beard might be gone, replaced with uneven lengths, but I'd recognise those black eyes anywhere. I'm too terrified to even breathe, let alone shout out.

'How did you find me?' I whisper.

'Your backpack.'

I bite my lip. 'I ... I told people about you,' I say. 'The police are looking for you already. You killed Vera.' I don't know what else to say. My body is frozen to the spot, but my eyes keep flicking to the stairs over to the left; my only escape route out of this basement.

'It's not like she didn't deserve it.'

'Are you here to kill me?' I whisper. I can't seem to drag my eyes away from the shimmering blade of the knife in his hand. Where the hell did he get that? Is that a knife from our kitchen? I can't be sure. How long has he been hiding down here? 'Were you in my room last night?' I ask.

Kevin grins at me as he flips the knife over in his hand. 'You see, Elle, I have a problem ... and that problem is you. You are the only person alive who has seen my face in the past twenty years. And I can't have you blabbing to people that I'm alive.'

I shake my head. 'It's too late. They already know.'

'That's a shame. It really is. You shouldn't have told them.'

'I don't understand. You're innocent. You didn't kill your parents. Vera did, so why are you worried about the police finding you? You killed Vera out of self-defence. I'm sure the cops would understand.'

Kevin steps closer, each footstep deliberately slow, like he's stalking me. 'Let's just say that Vera and I have a lot in common.'

He's close to me now; too close. I grab the nearest item on the shelf, which happens to be a piece of pipe with some sort of bolt at the end. I raise it above my head but feel utterly ridiculous in doing so. A knife against a pipe isn't really a fair fight, especially when the pipe is in the hands of a teenage girl versus a crazed lunatic.

'Stay back,' I say as strongly as I can, as I begin to shuffle towards the stairs. Kevin follows my every move.

He lunges and I run.

But my weak ankle collapses in a howl of agony as I reach the bottom of the stairs. I bash my knee against the hard concrete floor and turn around just as Kevin throws his body on top of mine. I kick out my legs but miss him as he slams his hand over my mouth, pushing down so hard all I can focus on is the pain.

Only muffled screams escape my mouth. Sometime during the scuffle, I drop the pipe. I hear it slide across the floor. Kevin leans his full weight on top of me, as he presses my body into the stairs, the wood digging into the small of my back.

'Twenty years in captivity does a lot to a man, Elle. I wasn't always like this.' My eyes widen. I try and shake my head, but I can barely move a muscle.

He raises the knife.

I pull my left knee up, slamming it into his groin. He

grunts and collapses, trying to curl into a foetal position. I wriggle free and manage to crawl away from him as he moans on the floor. He still has hold of the knife, but that's not what I'm aiming for. I grab the pipe, turn and slam it down on his head. A sharp crack signifies that I hit the mark.

Another grunt and he drops the knife, rolling over onto his back. I scramble towards it, grasp it and hold it out in front of me. He's not moving. And there's a lot of blood seeping from his head wound. I didn't mean to hit him so hard. The weird bolt at the end of the pipe must have sliced through his skull or fractured it badly.

Tears stream down my cheeks. Mum's already left. I'm frozen. What do I do? I've just killed someone ...

The front door opens.

'Only me! Forgot the shopping bags.'

'Mum! Come here! Quick! I'm in the basement!'

'Elle? What's wrong? Are you okay?'

I listen to the frantic footsteps above. My mum appears at the top of the stairs.

'Elle ... what are you ...' She stops when she sees me. 'Elle ... what's happened?'

'He attacked me ... I didn't mean to ... I think he's dead.'

Mum walks carefully down the stairs and steps around Kevin, who is crumpled at the bottom. She kneels next to me and gently lowers my outstretched hand with the knife, prising it from my grasp. 'Give it to me. It's okay, baby.'

'What are we going to do?'

'It will be okay. He was in our house. You did it out of self-defence.'

I nod, agreeing. 'Y-Yes.'

'The police are on their way and ...'

'No, Mum, no! They won't understand. They won't ...'

It all happens within an instant.

Mum has her back to Kevin, so she doesn't see him. He moves like lightning as he reaches for the pipe next to his outstretched hand.

'Mum! Look out!' I shriek.

Mum turns and spreads her arms out wide, protecting me. She shoves me to the side, grasping the knife in her left hand. Kevin throws himself forwards, probably too injured to realise his dreadful mistake as he impales himself on the knife and slumps forwards, his face only inches from Mum's.

'How dare you attack my daughter,' she says. 'How dare you.'

Kevin flicks his eyes at me for the last time and then he's still.

He's definitely dead this time.

Mum and I stay where we are, panting like dogs to catch our breaths. She moves first, placing the knife on the ground and then turning to look at me. She grasps my shoulders and scans me head to toe.

'Are you hurt?'

I shake my head.

Mum and I lock eyes.

'I should have done that to your father years ago,' she says.

The doorbell sounds upstairs.

'That's the police.'

My bottom lip trembles so badly I have to bite it to make it stop. 'I'm scared, Mum.'

She smiles as she strokes my hair. 'You don't ever have to be afraid again, Elle.'

The doorbell sounds again.

'Come on, let's go and talk to them and explain what happened.'

I nod and follow my mum upstairs to answer the door. I finally take a breath when I reach the top and look back down into the dim area. She's right. I don't have to be afraid anymore.

I no longer need the basement to be my safe space.

33

Willow
Five Years Ago

S he was out for one of her gentle afternoon strolls, enjoying the summer sunshine and the warmth on her face. She needed the fresh air, having been cooped up for hours in her room studying for her final school exams. Her boyfriend, Eric, was being frustratingly annoying and she needed space from him too. She didn't tell her father where she was going, nor did she take her mobile as she left the café her father owned and ran. It was called Carl's Place; not the most ingenious of names. She'd be back soon. She just needed some alone time.

Willow followed the path along the river, stopping to admire the flowers. She even spotted an otter family splashing in the water and watched them for a few minutes before continuing. She'd walked this way before, but never this far along. She knew Dawn House was situated just up the river, and there was never a good reason to get too close. She knew it was out of bounds and Vera didn't like trespassers on her land.

A twig snapped behind her, but when she turned to look there was no one on the path. Must have been a squirrel jumping from tree to tree. She'd seen plenty already during her walk.

But as she continued, the sound of footsteps was unmistakable.

'Who's there?' she called. 'Eric, is that you?'

Had he followed her? It would be typical of him to try and scare her. He was always doing that, and it was one of the things she had grown to hate about him. He liked to make her jump in terror, liked to surprise her by turning up unannounced, usually at a time that was very inconvenient. For weeks now, she'd been thinking of ending their relationship. She'd be going off to university soon, having been accepted into one in London. He wasn't going anywhere, as he was due to run his father's butcher's shop; a family business. He kept on and on at her that he wanted her to stay here with him, but she had no plans to stay here in the village forever. She wanted to see the world and Eric wasn't going to stop her.

Willow swallowed her fear and took a single step just as someone jumped out of the bushes behind her. 'Surprise!'

She screamed and tripped over her own feet, landing awkwardly on the dry path. 'Eric!'

'Sorry, babe, but you're too easy,' he said with a laugh as he helped her back up. She brushed the dirt from her legs and stamped her foot.

'Eric, I've told you I hate it when you jump out at me. What are you doing here? Were you following me?'

'I saw you leave the café and decided to see where you were going. You said you were staying in and studying for the rest of the day.'

'I changed my mind. I needed some fresh air.'

'I thought I'd join you.'

It was no coincidence that he'd seen her leave the café. He must have been watching from the shop. Why did he always have to know where she was? It was like he didn't trust her, even though she'd never given him any reason not to.

'Eric, I think we need to give each other some space.' It was now or never. She had to end things at some point – and he'd just provided her with the perfect opportunity.

A frown passed over his face. 'That's fine. Hey, I'll head back to the village if you want me to.'

'No, I ... I mean, I think we should break up. I don't want to see you anymore.'

Eric continued to frown, but then he laughed. 'Don't be stupid,' he said. 'You can't break up with me.'

'Yes, I can. I just did.'

Eric stepped closer; his fists suddenly clenched at either side of his body. 'I suggest you reconsider.'

Willow held her ground, but every muscle in her body was twitching, ready to flee at any second. He'd never hit her before, never laid a hand on her in an aggressive manner, but he was quite forceful, especially when they kissed. He'd always wanted to go further, but Willow kept saying no, and her apparent rejection would often piss him off.

'You are such a cocktease.'

'Excuse me?'

'You heard. You led me on all these months, and I've been nothing but patient with you, giving you the space and time you need, and now you're saying you don't want us to be together anymore.'

Willow lifted her chin a fraction of an inch. 'I should have broken up with you months ago. In fact, I should have never said yes to a date in the first place. Stacey was right about you.'

'Ha! Stacey's a cocktease too, but she loves the attention. Maybe I'll see if she wants to go out with me. Maybe she'd be more grateful.'

Willow didn't reply or move a muscle as Eric walked up to her. He lifted his hand and gently stroked her brown hair, twirling it through his fingers, then he brought it to his face and sniffed it and he ran the other hand along her side and down and over her hips.

'Tell me you want me to fuck you.'

Willow's stomach clenched. She stepped back and shoved him hard in the chest. 'Leave me alone!' Then she turned and started to run.

Behind her, Eric clenched his teeth as he bent down and grabbed a thick branch from the side of the path. He stormed after her, his footsteps thundering.

Willow screamed as her foot caught on a tree root and she sprawled to the ground, her head cracking against a rock.

Everything went dark, but she could still hear Eric shouting. She fought to keep her eyes open, but it was no use. Sharp pain engulfed her, swallowing her whole. She couldn't work out where she was or what was happening.

Footsteps sounded, but they weren't getting closer. They

were getting further away. Was Eric running to get help or was he running away in fear of what he'd done?

Her head pounded. Her vision swam.

Willow rolled over onto her stomach and slowly pushed herself to a kneeling position, gently touching her forehead. Her fingers came away covered in blood. It ran in a small river down the side of her cheek and was soaking into her dress.

'Help,' she whispered. 'Help.'

She looked around her, but Eric was gone. She was a long way from the village. The only place close by was Dawn House, just up the river. Maybe two hundred yards or so.

Willow's eyes streamed with tears as she crawled along the uneven path by the river, inching closer and closer to the house. She couldn't risk staying where she was in case Eric never came back with help. She didn't trust him, not even a little bit.

Several times Willow thought she was going to pass out, but she fought against the darkness, finally arriving at the grounds of Dawn House.

'Help!' she cried, but her voice was too weak, too quiet.

She'd met Vera several times and, despite her being a bit weird and withdrawn, she generally seemed nice, so Willow wasn't worried about being turned away. Vera wouldn't do that, would she?

Willow reached the front garden and pulled herself up to standing using a nearby fence post. She staggered towards the front door, collapsing against it. She bashed her fists against the wooden door as hard as she could, hoping and praying that Vera would answer. Her car was in the yard. She must be home. Where was she?

'Vera!'

Still no answer.

Willow took a deep breath before turning the doorknob and pushing the heavy door open. She stepped into the hallway, on the verge of passing out. She'd never been inside this house before. It was cold, slightly dirty and not very welcoming. She tried to listen out for any sounds, but the pounding in her head was so loud, she couldn't distinguish one noise from another.

A door was open in front of her, leading out of the hallway.

It looked like a basement door.

'Vera?' she called down into the dark.

'Who the hell are you!'

Willow spun round at the sharp tone, the movement making her head swim. Vera was standing in the doorway to the kitchen, holding two plates of food. Why two?

'I …' began Willow, but before she could get another word out, Vera had dropped the plates and rushed forwards, giving her a hard shove in the chest.

'Noooo!' Willow screamed as she toppled backwards down the stairs of the basement. Her head smashed into the concrete floor at the bottom.

She never woke up this time.

EPILOGUE

He needed to be quiet while he crept into his parents' bedroom. If either of them caught him in here, there would be hell to pay, and he couldn't take yet another beating. But he needed to find something, and he was almost certain it was in the drawer of his mother's dressing table. He'd watched her put it there a few weeks ago, so unless she'd moved it since then ...

The house was still, which made every creak in the floorboards sound louder than usual. Vera was in bed, having got sick with the flu several days ago, and now it was their birthday and he wanted to give her something to cheer her up, although his true motive behind the gesture was much more sinister.

As he slowly pulled open the drawer, he caught a

glimpse of something shiny. It was what he'd come here for. His father had bought it several months ago for their mother; it had cost a lot of money, more money than they could afford to spend on something so utterly useless. She opened up this drawer every night before she went to bed, using the hairbrush inside to brush her hair so she was bound to notice it was missing. The brush was right next to the bracelet. It had to work.

Kevin picked up the silver bracelet and slipped it into his pocket.

He wanted to give it to Vera, not as a kind gesture, but as a catalyst to cause their father to attack her. Not to kill her, although it was likely she would get badly hurt. It wouldn't take a lot for him to lose his mind. Plus, he'd had a lot to drink tonight. Kevin had seen to that as well, handing him a new bottle of beer each time he finished one.

No, his plan wasn't to get rid of Vera. It was to get rid of their father.

Vera may have been weak with fever, but she could turn at any minute.

He was scared of her, always had been, ever since he'd woken to find her standing over his bed. But he was more afraid of their father. He had to go.

It would be better this way.

His plan was perfect.

His father would attack Vera.

Vera would snap and kill him.

Then, Kevin would be free.

THANK YOU FOR READING

Did you enjoy reading *Don't Tell a Soul*? Please consider leaving a review on Amazon. Your review will help other readers to discover the novel.

ACKNOWLEDGMENTS

This is my first traditionally published book, having been self-published for the past three and a half years, so I'll start by thanking each and every one of you, my readers, who have supported me from the beginning of my author career even before my first book was out. Your belief and support in me have been invaluable and I really do appreciate all of you. Thank you for continuing to be here on my author journey as I enter the traditional publishing world.

I must also say a huge thank you to Connal Orton at Inkubator Books, who emailed me out of the blue in December 2023 and told me he saw potential in my writing and offered me a contract with Inkubator. He and Brian Lynch really helped me understand what the publisher was looking for in a psychological thriller and helped me hone and develop the plot of *Don't Tell a Soul* to what you see today. I'm extremely proud of this first book with Inkubator and I have Connal and Brian to thank for having faith in me!

Thank you to my dad, twin sister, Alice and best friend, Katie, for being my cheerleaders from the start of my career, even when I wrote books in my room as a teenager, dreaming of the day I'd be a published author. They always believed in me and my writing.

Thanks to my amazing self-published author friends who I've met along the way. Despite now stepping into the world of traditional publishing, they continue to have my back, support and shout about my career and accomplishments, and it's the most amazing community to be a part of.

Lastly, thank you to all the team at Inkubator Books who have copy edited, proofread, formatted and delivered this book to the highest of standards, and to everyone on the team who does the marketing, ARC books, book tours and all the other things that make a book release the best it can be. It's been very surreal stepping back from having to do it all myself. Having a great, talented team behind me is something I will cherish and never take for granted because it's a hell of a lot of work!

ABOUT THE AUTHOR

Jessica Huntley is an author of dark and twisty psychological thrillers, which often focus on mental health topics and delve deep into the minds of her characters. She has a varied career background, having joined the Army as an Intelligence Analyst, then left to become a Personal Trainer. She is now living her life-long dream of writing from the comfort of her home, while looking after her young son and her disabled black Labrador. She enjoys keeping fit and drinking wine (not at the same time).

www.jessicahuntleyauthor.com
Sign up for her newsletter on her website and receive a free short story.

ALSO BY JESSICA HUNTLEY

Printed in Great Britain
by Amazon